FOUR LEAF CLOVER

Jacquie Crowther

FOUR LEAF CLOVER

For Noo-Noo

Jacquie Crowther
Profile

Since the age of ten Jacquie Crowther has been creating prize winning poetry and paintings, based on her love of all things natural.

For most of her adult life Jacquie has been accompanied by poor mental health and has navigated her way across some arduous emotional territory. Now, embracing her individuality, Jacquie writes with compassion, honesty and an incredible insight into the skills and strengths of some remarkable women who have travelled with her.

Jacquie now lives in Berkshire, where she spends her time tending her menagerie of pets, caring for her family and learning to love herself.

Reviews

Email:Jacquie1crowther@gmail.com
Creativecrazy.home.blog

When the day finally dawns
And I'm no longer here
To laugh with you, and to hold you near

You won't have to travel so far away
To find me ready, waiting to play.

Let your body or mind take you down to the sea,
Wherever you turn, you'll always see me.
In the sparkling waves, as they lap on the sand
Gently caressing, I'm holding your hand.

Let the warm rays of sunlight soak into your skin
And my perpetual love will come flooding in.
In the gentle sea breeze, as it brushes your ears
I'm whispering your name, calming your fears.

Turn your face to the wild and blustery wind
And I'll ruffle your hair until I find
A way to uplift your quivering chin,
Dry your briny tears, so your peace may begin.

So if the day finally dawns when you can't see me here,
And the storm subsides, but no rainbow appears,
Believe and find comfort that down by the sea
My Spirit lives on, happy, wild and free,
Waiting to help you feel closer to me.

Jacquie Crowther 2001

THE WHYS AND WHERE-FORE'S

I don't claim to be the author of an epic novel, fit for the big screen, but I *am* the author of *Four Leaf Clover*. For as long as I can remember I have wanted to write a book. Along the way I have dabbled in poetry, drawing and painting and now I have finally put pen to paper. *Four Leaf Clover* is a tale of some of the women in my life who have been an inspiration to me, and no doubt to others, and is my interpretation of the legacies they have each passed on to me. Motivation, encouragement, nurturing and love (with a small dose of chastising) all existed in abundance throughout my childhood, even if I couldn't always see or feel it. Although I sometimes feel quite melancholy about the efforts made to bestow all of these upon me, which I surely failed to acknowledge at the time, I revel at the fact that I am able to recall so many memories which were shared within the folds of some outstandingly strong women in my life. It's this which makes me a firm believer in the notion that whatever experience you give your child, from the very day they are born, could be a future memory for him or her. We have no way of knowing what our amazing minds will file away, a snippet of a story, wise words or even harsh and unkind words. Evoking a feeling associated with a sensory experience. Whatever it might be, however it might manifest itself, you can influence your child's life and values for longer than you might possibly imagine.

Of course there are strong women in every family and there are some precious women still alive in mine. Life deals them some unbelievable tough hands at times and they survive. But more than that, they manage, soldier on, take the bull by the horns, however you want to describe it. I prefer to say they use all four chambers of their hearts. As unique women, these four chambers each contain immeasurable amounts of courage, love, strength and compassion. As unique women, they each draw on what's in their hearts in times of trouble, hoping they will be able to cope and be strong for other people. And, as unique women, that's exactly what they do without even realising the enormity of their achievements. If pride really does come before a fall, look out for me when I go a-tumbling because I'm proud to be one of the women in my family. There are so many "wise sayings" about how futile worrying is but the most poignant one I like to remember was, I believe, said by Mother Theresa: with acceptance comes peace.

Some might say that it is sad how I waited so long to write this, my foremothers never getting to read it, but it's exactly the opposite. The time is right for me to share these memories, not because these lovely women are no longer alive, not because I feel the need to commemorate them, and not because it massages my ego. The time is right – for me. The woman who feels so blessed to have known, loved and be loved by such beautiful people. The woman who now embraces the opportunity to be the custodian of an absolutely priceless heirloom – The Apron Strings.

ACKNOWLEDGEMENTS

First and foremost, although it may seem obvious, I need to mention the four "real women" who very kindly provided me with the material – by way of experiences – to even contemplate writing this book. Whilst it is my personal interpretation of how our lives intertwined, the characters are based on four amazing people.

In no particular order, they are both of my grandmothers and my own wonderful mum, all of whom were called Irene! This initially led me to choose pseudonyms and it also made it easier for me to write (and to read). They were, namely, Irene Maude Earl, Irene Davis and Irene Margaret Earl. Born into very different families, and in extremely different circumstances, they were brought together by something far more powerful than fate. And, whilst they made indelible marks on me as a child, in their absence they continue to feature in my life - etching deeper into my being that those around me can surely feel their presence.

Not only do I need to acknowledge these three women but there have, and continue to be, men who have supported and encouraged me throughout my life. Firstly there's my dear old dad, Bob. He has always been an inspiration to me and encouraged me in so many ways. As a child and teenager, he taught me things from appreciating the wonder of wild birds, riding pillion on a motorbike and home brewed cider! Plus much, much more.

Also, without them always realising it there have been men in my life who have also enabled me to express myself by realising the creativity fed by my imagination and perceptions of the world. Namely, my ever suffering husband, Paul. He has been patient in allowing me the space and time to face my demons and embrace the person I found myself to be along the way. I would love to say I'm grateful for his understanding but this would be far from reality – he tolerates me, albeit with little understanding, and lets me be when there's turmoil all around us. I love Paul.

I also love my handsome, intelligent, funny, awesome and all round perfect son, Tom. He would never forgive me if I didn't describe him in this way, using his own words, but he really is amazing. From when he was a toddler Tom has been in tune with me and my feelings. From instinctively knowing when I need a hug to sensing when my day had been particularly stressful, he would often take it upon himself to massage the tension from my neck. Oh yes, I'm proud and so thankful for his love and encouragement and the way he sees the world – even if he has been known to wear rose-tinted Ray-bans!

With an innocence beyond comprehension, my wonderful grandson, Noah, has been and continues to be a true inspiration in my life and in my determination to finish this book. Whilst it has been my mind which has been less than healthy, Noah faces unimaginable challenges with his health and development, and will for the rest of his life. I feel useless when I try and think of how I can't help him physically. I feel so sad that I can't fix his medical conditions. So all I can do is to help him feel the love and encouragement he always gives to others. Noah, I believe you are achieving so much already with a charisma which attracts and helps all those who meet you, without you being aware of it.

Hand in hand with my thanks to those I have already mentioned, I treasure the love and encouragement I continue to receive from my amazing friends. Again, "in no particular order" I would like to bottle the support and motivation from Haro – the problem-solver – who's friendship gave me an insight to a world which took us from bar to bar, country to country and provided me with a safe haven for many years. Whilst we still haven't gotten round to producing all of the life-saving inventions which we created over our bowls of porridge, Haro showed me that all dreams *are* possible. As well as Haro, there are some friends who certainly have stood the test of time. Through true friendship Paola and Esther have been a constant source of support in darker times, laughter in lighter times and down-right craziness most of the rest of the times! We haven't always shared political views, or a love of aubergines, or even a penchant for eating whole limes. But we have shared a genuine love of good friends and valued the importance of showing it. There's no doubt that I have told them how much of an inspiration they are to me, but I will tell them again, and again and again.

There are people in all of our lives who seem to believe in us far more than we believe in ourselves. Not only parents and relatives. Lynn is one such person. I know she won't agree, but I owe her so much for her faith in me, encouragement, understanding and for the numerous opportunities to try my best! Making her an honorary member of my family is just the beginning.

And then there's Wendy! I'm absolutely positive that Wendy has helped in my "rebirth" with her love, support and a healthy balance of congratulations and criticism. She joined me on a journey of some extreme highs and lows by encouraging me to be the person I was frightened to unleash, in case I didn't like who I was. Don't worry if you don't understand this, just accept me the way Wendy does.

I am acutely aware that I haven't given mention to the remarkable women who are very much present in my family today.
Throughout my whole life I have had a special relationship with my favourite auntie. In so many ways, we have travelled down the same paths – at different times – and, likewise, we have each had some very different experiences. But I know and believe that auntie Susan has been one of the most influential women in my life. The way she has shown her love for me has never wavered, nor has my love for her. Whilst I really want to acknowledge the impact our relationship has made on my life, I also want you to know that the way she has always nurtured my individuality has really helped me to believe in myself. It's this sense of self belief which resonates to underpin the way Susan makes me feel that I have a right to be here and that I actually belong here.

The youngest women-to-be in my life who deserve a significant mention are my awesome grand-daughters. Abbie never ceases to amaze me with her simplistic outlook on life and her lack of any sense of urgency. As a stunning and loving young woman, it is her view of me as a bit of a weirdo which warms my heart the most. She accepts my little peccadilloes, she tolerates my dress sense and openly laughs at the way I morph together my unwanted clothes into something which I wear – in public. Abbie almost sails through life and never fails to help me focus on the here and now. Being comfortable with each other has helped me be comfortable with myself. I'm so blessed to have known her since the very minute she was born and to watch her evolve into a beautiful, inspiring young woman. From the closeness she feels with her family to the bond she shares with Pinkie, Abbie is surrounded by love which only reflects that which she exudes.

No, I haven't forgotten Millie! Even at the tender age of five, Millie gives me an abundance of the knowledge, memories and motivation which I have needed to enable me to write anything, let alone this book. To say she is amazing is an understatement. Never failing to entertain me with her free style dance to the most moving music, or educate me with her outstanding vocabulary, Millie really is an inspiration. With her wild imagination, she continues to be a creative, kind, and clever individual who just loves alliteration! And with her "self-styled" dress sense we are peas in a pod.   I'm grateful for the relationships I have with all of my grandchildren, they truly are gifts to be cherished. They each give me so much, in very different ways, and have contributed to my writing in ways for which I can find no words.

Finally, there's my precious daughter, Tori. I found my voice when she was born. Nothing comes close to the love a mother feels for her children and it can only be appreciated by mothers, themselves. As a daughter, Tori gave me a reason to get up in the morning- as well as to go to bed at night! A clever and inquisitive little girl who only stopped talking when she fell asleep, never ceased to amaze me. I grew up the minute she was born and was instantly overwhelmed with a sense of responsibility. As I held her for the first time I became acutely aware that I wasn't only holding a new born baby, but I was holding the essence of a woman. I admit to feeling a proud mum, not only then but as she grew into a woman. Those memories and experiences are priceless and I only hope she will be moved, loved and inspired as a mum herself. Being blessed with something as miraculous as a child is amazing. But knowing the *woman* your daughter has become is phenomenal.

Table of Contents

1   MAUD – THE WOMAN

Never usually affording herself the time for reflection, Maud found the act of reminiscing quite alien. Yet somehow she felt the need for looking back on her life, as she sat in the calmness of the eve of her wedding. Another indulgent episode. Her memory was far-reaching and, as far as she knew, as accurate as her father's watch when it came to meal times. There were times when she could have benefited from a little hindsight but it had always managed to elude her, wafting out of the window, on the breeze of every-day life. Whilst Maud didn't forget the times when she (and everyone around her) toiled through what seemed to be never ending strife, she knew that dwelling on her past was futile. Masking her melancholy, and feelings which loosely resembled self-pity, Maud girded herself with hope and hanky – ready to face whatever the future might, or might, not hold.

For her, and virtually all of the women Maud knew, marriage was always on the cards as she was raised with the traditional belief that that's what women do in the 1920's. A shrewd and clever girl, she was more than capable of finding meaningful work which would allow her to contribute financially to the household. However, if it was a matter of qualifications, she might struggle to find employment other than in "service". Now - that was something Maude was definitely qualified for. Even though she had only spent one day *actually* working in somebody else's house, Maud had undoubtedly earned a future out of slaving for a pittance of a wage. Although, in truth, Maud had never once thought of her role within her family as slaving. She had never had a wage packet or a smart uniform, or even a company issue pin with their name written in brass. Her every waking moment spent caring for others was the right path for her – God's will. Following the early death of her mother and baby sister – to the all-too-common tuberculosis – she had found herself raising her seven brothers, until they – in turn – found themselves providing for expanding families of their own. So the notion of Maud going out to seek work was never even debated.

There had been times when she hoped and prayed that there was at least some truth in the adage "as son is a son 'til he takes him a wife but a daughter's a daughter for the rest of her life". If her marriage were to be blessed with children, Maud found a tiny piece of her hoping she would have a daughter. God willing.

As a child and young adult, Maud had deeply loved and admired her mother but today she thought of the legacy she had left Maud in the guise of her surviving siblings and her father. Almost in the blink of an eye, she had been swept from being a sibling to a surrogate mother, from a child to a woman and, again, the topic wasn't up for discussion. Her father definitely upheld the view that children should be seen and not heard (unless it was to call him to the table for tea). Try as he might, he found balancing appropriate discipline with boisterous fun as easy as balancing a raw egg on a tennis racquet. In his mind, boys should be boys along with the resulting noise. There was no doubt in Maud's mind that they were each made of slugs and snails and puppy-dog tails. All ingredients which could be found in abundance in the back alley (maybe not the puppy-dog tails). The sugar and spice which Maud was "made of" were far more difficult for her father to source. Therefore, it seemed to her, the responsibility to find and preserve that sugar and spice fell upon her own fair shoulders. This reflected the stark reality that, Maud's father was also thrown into the alien role of single parent, which he couldn't possibly have predicted when fathering nine children.

Maud made no space or time for resentment or regret as the house had been a hustling, bustling hive of activity with never a dull moment. Some of her relatives had hinted that her mother had, in fact, lost her life to an ectopic pregnancy but – not really knowing what that meant – Maud chose to believe otherwise. Even as a young adolescent, it seemed to Maud that anything to do with a pregnancy couldn't possibly have taken the life of her younger sister too. It had fleetingly occurred to Maud that for every conversation she had over-heard (or occasionally been party to) there were many more which had escaped her via hushed voices or trapped in a room behind a hurriedly closed door, for which the key remained firmly in her imagination.

Of course there were times when she felt such fantasies were something of a burden to her young mind. As if she didn't have enough on her plate, without trying to fathom out whether the memories she had of her beautiful mother were so entwined with her wildest imaginings that she was being duped by her own beliefs. Try as she might, Maud found it virtually impossible to separate this muddled string of thoughts. What if she just caressed the twine enough to unfurl the ply just fraction of a fray? Would she find a paradise of a peaceful country garden carpeted with a myriad of precious gems, the calming cerulean blue of forget-me-nots; the garishly cheerful orange of montbretias, craning for their share of sunlight; the deepest indigo and canary yellow blending across the wild pansies, velvety to the touch? Or maybe an imposing haberdashery displaying reams of silk, lace and organza, in every imaginable exotic colour and hue in God's own palette? An emporium of textures, ribbons of satin just waiting to be caressed; contrasting like braille of linen and lace lying side by side; hand-painted buttons of any size she could possibly want, in more shapes than Maud could name. These images remained Maud's fantasies for two very good reasons. Not only were the wares of the haberdashery safely displayed in highly polished, mahogany cabinets which towered over virtually every customer, firmly out of the reach of anyone who were tempted to trace their fingers over the luxurious fabrics. But, Maud also knew that the Devil makes work for idle hands and she felt she had enough to do without the Devil adding to her list of chores. Her solution? To tuck her imagination up tightly in the bed linen and wear gloves when she went out!

Maud had been born in a Victorian two- up two-down terraced house. Whilst it had an outside toilet, which was shared with spiders and other tenants, it was hardly suitable for her parents to raise an ever growing family. As sure as eggs is eggs, if one of the children needed to "go" then they all needed to "go". In the peachy glow of dawn, each child scuttled to the brick shed. Nightshirt under the chin, they each did their business and scuttled back inside. The youngest of them was treated to the privilege of sluicing the pan with the ice cold contents of the water butt. Whilst the oldest enjoyed the privilege of reaching the little coal fire quick enough to nab a prime position. The chore of tearing newspaper into squares was allocated on a rota system. The early morning emptying of the orange cocktail from the china Poe was also undertaken in rotation. Being the mother of such a brood had some benefits as the less popular jobs could be delegated or traded for the first place in the dinner queue! Hungry children were as plentiful as chores.

As luck would have it another terraced house in Dudley Road had become available at a most fortuitous time so they duly ferried their limited chattels across the street. The new house had three bedrooms, its own flushing toilet (but no bathroom), a scullery kitchen and two ample reception rooms. This all led from a long narrow hall, which appeared to Maud bigger than the entire old terraced house.

Maybe it was as a result of living in the previous cramped conditions, but the front reception room became a parlour, used only for high days and holidays as well as very important discussions between adults as they adopted the "not in front of the children" stance. This room eventually became suitably furnished with carpet in the middle of the parquet tiled floor, on which sat three varied soft armchairs, almost like a hospital waiting room – another place which required conversation in hushed voices. Over the years it was to become the room where they put the "best furniture" and anything which could be considered of worth or had rare sentimental value.

Such humble beginnings with a reasonable share of financial difficulties seemed normal as Maud was growing up. Whilst other people may have had a few extra pennies to go to the Lord Walsley pub with, or – unbelievably - to buy themselves a trim new blouse, Maud considered it frivolous and careless to fritter away such hard-earned money. After all, she hadn't spent a considerable amount of her own childhood perfecting her domestic skills to pay someone else for something she could do perfectly well herself. The ever-doting sister had formed her outlook on such things when she was very young. In fact, pride of place on the mantel piece stood a sepia photograph of Maud and Albert, one of her younger brothers. It had been taken in a professional studio by Charlesworth & Co in Manor Parade in Southall and she was dressed in a dark dress (probably grey) with a white pinafore. Her ringlets gently framing her small face, made to look even smaller by her shining brown eyes and rather demure smile. Sitting straight-backed, on a satin-covered chaise longue, Maude looked every bit the young lady, despite being only six-years-old. Standing beside her was Albert in his romper suit shorts, looking equally as angelic, both in their buttoned leather boots. Perfect for the family album if it wasn't for the huge bow which sat, like a freshly preened swan, on Albert's chest. Albert had found a water biscuit somewhere which he had smeared all down the front of his Sunday best clothes. It was far from the trend for 1911 but Maud had come to the rescue with her resourcefulness by removing the sash from her dress to fashion a cravat-like cummerbund. In fact, Maud had since heard that Sears in America had produced a catalogue with children modelling the latest in fashion but she was certain that none of their outfits would measure up to the unique suit her brother was sporting as he posed for the camera. Her pride creeping in under the guise of her sense of humour.

Sitting at the table in an unusually quiet house, Maud dismissed the notion that maybe the fading photograph was indication that other things had been "hidden" or dressed up to resemble something more perfect. With little or no privacy in the house, and being the only female among eight men, Maud quickly realised that there simply hadn't been enough space, time or inclination to put on an act for all of her life so far. In fact it was quite the opposite.

She remembered and valued the belief that you shouldn't air your dirty linen in public as much as you were "careful" about becoming the subject of the local gossip. Maud wondered if this had been a nugget of fact from her grandfather or a practice which they had adopted from her teenage-years. It wasn't the easiest achievement to get her youngest brother to believe that walls didn't actually have real ears, but it had been a clever slogan to discourage people from gossiping during the war. One which she pledged to retain and applied within her pending marriage – looking forward to finally having something and someone of her own. Not that she begrudged caring for the men in the family and she felt the butterflies stirring up guilt at the prospect of gaining a new sir name. At the thought of becoming Mrs Maud Lord, she casually wrote her new signature on the back of the brown paper wage packet her father had left for her to reuse. Mrs Lord sounded so much better than Maud Lord and she smiled as she wondered if there would be even more teasing than that which her brothers had subjected her to since she became engaged. Try as she might, she couldn't be sure whether the two words had a meaning in London rhyming slang - but she sincerely hoped not.

Maud was no stranger to teasing and high jinks. As they became older her brothers graduated into a private club of men - having a secret mission statement of "It is a member's responsibility to maximise every opportunity to cause confusion, angst and bemusement to Maud, regardless of cost and custom". Although she hadn't always found their antics amusing, as she had been the subject of most of them, and wistfully recalling some of them brought a soft smile to her face, as she indulged herself in a second cup of tea. Her memory had been known to blur facts but she had no difficulty bringing to mind "the soap incident". As busy men, some had occasionally been known to make unreasonable demands and bark orders at Maud, mostly when they were hungry or wanted her to fill the old tin bath for them so they could scrub the working week's dirt off themselves. They even complained when she rationed the use of the coal tar soap as she would pride herself on being careful with any money they had. Cutting each bar in half saved money but the little pink blocks created an inferior lather as they made their escape from the grasp of huge and clumsy hands.

So it was only a matter of time before Maud retaliated. And, when she did, Maud did it in her own unique style. Such was her anger that the usual unassuming and frugal sister very "kindly" made her brother Tom a sandwich before he had the chance to demand it. With the p's and q's he was raised with Tom duly thanked Maud before taking a seat at the table with his lunch. Tom hadn't noticed that Maud had taken herself out to the garden – despite the chilly autumn weather. Tom hadn't noticed that the sandwich was much thicker and miss-shapen in the centre. Tom hadn't noticed the sweet perfumed aroma of his sandwich. Tom did notice, as his pearly whites sank into the thinly sliced bread, the sickening flavour of the pink cake of carbolic soap Maud had so thoughtfully nestled inside his sandwich. Tom did notice the way the soap quickly formed a slick of whale oil and the antiseptic of petroleum on his tongue. Tom also noticed, for several days to come, the way his teeth continued to emit that same taste as it worked its' way out of the grooves and grain of his now pink teeth! Malice couldn't have been further away from her mind when Maud chuckled about it to herself – later and in private.

Such fond memories of playfulness danced around Maud's mind in the hour or so that she had been sitting there, thinking and contemplating how her past will be so intertwined with her future. Whilst that seemed a logical thought, somewhere in her mind she felt a need to make it her responsibility to capture and filter the most important and useful memories so that she might create space for new ones. The trouble was, how was she to know which bits of knowledge, which skills and lessons would she need as a wife – and maybe a mother? As Maud was not one for dithering and dallying in such matters, she promptly cast aside these worries and, as she tied her floral pinnie around her trim waist she set to the real task in hand.

Making her own wedding dress had been a forgone conclusion for Maud as she certainly had the skills required for such fine needlework. However, despite having little or no funds for a stylish wedding gown, which she felt was a huge unnecessary extravagance, she had been persuaded by her father to buy a new gown - if only to keep him happy. When it mattered, he was still the proud father of a wonderful daughter and wanted the best he could afford for her.

A kind of sadness washed over her as she took her sewing box on her knee. Lined with soft red satin, padded so to provide a huge pin cushion, it had belonged to her mother. She had been so cruelly denied such pleasures as spending hours teaching Maud how to sew or knit, in order to ensure the family were as smartly dressed as they could be. With her life cut so short, her mother may not have imparted her domestic knowledge verbally but Maud had inherited her sense of pride as she watched her mother darn and sew for her siblings. With freshly-washed hands, the five-year-old Maud had been allowed to touch all the trimmings and bows which her mother kept in her sewing box. It looked more like a treasure trove to Maud as she let the bric-brac wind through her chubby fingers and wonder at the way her mother passed the cotton through the eye minute of a needle with such skill and precision. Now that the sewing box was hers' she saw that the delicate snippets of ribbons and knicker elastic were bound with her mothers' patience and determination instead. An array of random buttons, lying ready and willing to secure the love with which her mother had collected them. These qualities had carried her through some challenging times, and would continue to do so for Maud for many years to come.

Maud might not be making her own wedding gown but, with less than twenty-four hours to spare, her delft fingers would weave their magic into smartening up her brothers for the big day. It meant hours starching collars, straightening wayward buttons and altering the length of the trousers which had been passed down (and passed down again) from one brother to another. They also took pride in themselves and the way they dressed – totally unaware of how expertly Maud applied her flair for invisible mending. Well turned out and fit for any of the seven brides which would be needed for the seven brothers. Tom ready and fit for the camera – without water biscuit smudged across his suit. He had even lost his unruly curls which had, in fact, made him resemble Shirley Temple more than the handsome young man who stood tall (ish) before her. Of her seven brothers, Tom had remained something of a favourite, a fact which he knew to the point of exploitation.

Having made their vows in the presence of all their nearest and dearest, a dapper Mr & Mrs Edward Lord stepped from the church into mediocre sunshine. Maud felt like a damsel, on the arm of her knight in shining armour and it could have been a full blown thunder storm for all she cared. Standing at least fourteen inches taller than her, Edward may have seemed quite imposing to some but to his bride and all who knew him, he was the perfect gentleman and she felt honoured to be married to him. In retrospect, her fathers' decision to buy her a new dress had indeed made her feel important, if not deserving. Seeing the smiling faces of their guests celebrating their special day was reward enough for Maud. The wedding gifts which accompanied them were gratefully received but it was the warmth and love in abundance which cemented the moment in her memory forever.

Frivolity was definitely not her style but she couldn't keep the glint from her dark brown eyes as she drank in the atmosphere of such a huge family celebration, not to mention the diamonds and gold which adorned her tiny hands. Nothing could have been farther from her thoughts than the reality that, one day, Maud would leave this stunning ring to her only Granddaughter who would treasure it, wearing it with almost as much pride as Maud felt this day. Maud had made her vows earnestly, in the presence of God, and had no doubt that she would love, honour and obey her Edward until death do they part.

Cloaked in the serenity of the church service, she savoured her inner tranquillity as their friends and dearly loved savoured the contrasting hullabaloo of celebrations.

It was tradition in 1929 to save the top tier of the wedding cake to make into a Christening cake when a couple started a family. With only enough ingredients for one tier, Maud silently prayed that this wasn't an omen for her and Edward. The thought of not having children (maybe not as many as her parents had) was not one which Maud or Edward would have entertained, despite being a subject which they had not yet been brave enough to broach. Growing up with a family such as hers, Maud knew full well how babies were conceived – the husband and wife slept in the same bed and before you know it the wife is "in the family way". Now Maud was far from stupid but, like so many of her peers of the time, pregnancy and the bare mechanics of it were a taboo subject. Love and respect were key ingredients in a marriage, she knew this much as it had been demonstrated so well by her own parents. As with so many aspects of marriage, it seemed to her that this type of education just didn't happen and therefore she didn't know what to expect on her wedding night. As a wise and maternal woman, Maud used her determination and pragmatic ways to make sure she did what "she was supposed to" and started to pray that they would soon be blessed with baby Lord.

And so it was…. With the love and respect of Edward, in 1938 Maud found herself "in the family way" - just as all of her relatives had predicted. She even dared to be happier than the day she had married Edward, in all her finery. Now she sat, at the same old table, with Edward by her side as they shared the news with her father and equally proud Grandfather. Living under the same roof as them seemed a natural thing to do and it worked well for all of them. After all, as her brothers each lived and loved and left, there was more room for everyone. Her grandfather was still – and would continue to be for many years to come – the man of the house. Maud and Edward had their own room in the slightly less industrious house than when all of her brothers lived at home and she was able to continue to care for her beloved father as well as be as dutiful as wife as could be. It really was wedded bliss, even though she had to endure the fog of smoke which sat around the room when her father was home. A smell which caused her to run for the scullery and fresh air in the early stages of pregnancy. Woodbines were a significant part of his life and one of his "little pleasures". Although he quite enjoyed a couple of drinks in the Lord Wolseley along the road. Or maybe a game of cards or two with his sons. Of course Maud also played cards, better than some of her brothers, but smoking was an absolute no. Like coffee, it was for "strumpets" who flaunted themselves in the public bars of the local pubs or Working Men's Club. This wasn't a false front she put on, it was a quality of the respectable young lady Maud was.

2 IVY – THE WOMAN

Like her siblings, Ivy had been blessed with above average intelligence and succeeded well at school. Her favourite subject was mathematics, closely followed by English – although she often felt she was cheating in this subject as it was the only language she knew. Along-side English, came drama as a close favourite, but mainly because she enjoyed the end of year productions. Her final performance, before leaving school at fifteen, had been Charles Dickens' Little Dorrit, in which she played Amy in the title role. The enjoyment this gave her wasn't based on a desire to perform in front of an adoring audience, or just show off. In a bazaar way was merely the opportunity it gave her to be herself. Being part of such a close family often meant that her individuality became diluted by her role within the family. Having to try and understand Dickens' language was a fair trade-off for the time she had to herself – ironically playing the part of a girl who was growing up in a close and complex family.   Now, all of that seemed a lifetime away as she prepared excitedly for her first day in her new job. Having passed the audition – which some might call an interview - Ivy had secured a job in a local accountant's office. Not being work shy, she was keen to be earning some money so that she contribute to the household bills, as well as spending more time indulging in her main passion for swimming.

As a child, not only had she been a key member of the cast of several productions, Ivy had represented Oxford Gardens School in the regional schools swimming galas for a number of years. She really enjoyed diving as well as being adept at various swimming strokes. However, synchronised swimming was her absolute favourite. Every Saturday Ivy would be the first in the queue at the Lancaster Road swimming baths, with the exception of the women waiting in line with their laundry. Most of the local women would beat the early morning queues when they opened at 8 am on a Monday, but there were a few who worked in the week so Saturday it was. Ivy took their incessant chatter as a form of the excitement she felt as they queued.

There were, in fact, four pools in the building, which stood on the corner of Lancaster Road and Silchester Road. Although there was a pool reserved for women only, there were two pools exclusively for men to use. The larger of the two was the men's 2nd class pool which was slightly smaller than the main pool with the high- diving boards. Smaller still was the men's 3rd class pool which had minute curtained changing cubicles by the side of the pool. Ivy and her sister Dot had been known to take a sneaky peek through the cubicle wall cavity on occasion but they had been chased off when their giggling had echoed around the pool, catching the attention of some of the swimmers and attendants. They conceded that the reason was probably due to the fact that this pool was reserved for men who could not afford a bathing costume and were permitted, therefor, to swim entirely naked!

Most of the time Ivy swam in the main pool, which was reported to be Olympic size but it was the added attraction of the diving boards which captured her interest most. Competing in the Olympics wasn't exactly one of her ambitions, local competitions were enough for her. The local swimming club also met and trained in this pool as it had a more distinct deep end and a spectator's gallery. It was here that Ivy spent virtually all of her free time trying to perfect her synchronised swimming skills. There was no other activity which could give her such a sense of freedom, grace and total lack of self-consciousness whilst at the same time providing a source of exercise. Ivy would revel in any opportunity to don her swimming cap – fetching with pink rubber roses on top – and dive into the water where she and her fellow swimming club members would perform a water-based ballet to music. In the pool her agility was so far removed from any physical activity she tried to engage in on dry land. Having contracted polio as a child, Ivy was left with a rolling gait due to one of her legs being considerably shorter than the other. Even though she was "lucky" enough to have a built up shoe she was proud of the fact that her disability didn't prevent her from doing anything she wanted except dancing on terra firma.

Undefeated by any physical limitations, and with equal abandonment, Ivy simply refocused her love of musical movement to singing (surprisingly tuneful). An ability to change the direction of her path in life, stumbling along the winding routes was pathed with determination would carry her through some of life's trials and tribulations.

At a height of 5ft 9", Ivy often attracted attention for more positive reasons. During summer months she would develop a deep olive tan and, with her dark wavy hair she almost looked Mediterranean. Her stunning blue eyes appeared as deep lavender against her sun kissed skin, and there was no denying that she turned the heads of many an admirer. As a growing teenager, Ivy tried her utmost to remain slightly aloof where men were concerned. In fact, it was Dot who was more likely to respond playfully to flirtatious advances from men so they often toyed with those who paid them attention whenever they were out together. On occasion, Dot was quite protective of Ivy and would ward off any unwanted advances. At the same time she would also see the fun and games they had together as an opportunity or her to try and impart some of her knowledge of the stronger sex. Not that she was particularly experienced but Dot had the most confidence out of the two and felt that she was a better judge of character than the ever-trusting Ivy.

It was during one of their swimming trips together when they had decided to go into the main pool – despite it costing twice as much as the 4d for the women's pool. Not only did they have lanes to swim in but the changing cubicles were in the gallery and they could watch the other swimmers for a while first. However, several people also stood and watched over the railings and, on this occasion, Dot noticed one young man paying them more attention than she would have liked. She had seen him there before and he always seemed to observe people without actually swimming himself. Whilst there were no rules against this, Dot found it a little bit odd and secretly questioned his motives. Ivy, however, had started to enjoy the attention he gave her and sometimes sneaked a side-ways glance at him as they swam up and down. Attempting to improve her speed and style in case he was actually a scout for other swimming clubs, or a professional swimmer himself, made the lengths she swam even more purposeful. She even wondered if he had some kind of aversion or allergy to water, as he never went in the pool, but decided it was probably because he didn't want to risk his hair tonic getting washed away.

There was an air of cockiness about him which Dot distinctly disapproved of but Ivy told herself it was more like an attractive confidence. Although they had never yet spoken to him that was about to change. As Dot and Ivy made their way out of the women's cubicles, with tousled wet hair, they noticed him loitering by the exit. One minute he was standing alone and the next he was by their side and asking if they enjoyed their swim. Dot was definitely not as impressed as Ivy and she told him that they weren't in the habit of talking to strangers, a haughty air in her voice. At this, he offered his hand and introduced himself as Jonny Freeman. Before Dot could deter her, Ivy had shaken his warm hand and offered both of their names – adding that she had enjoyed her swim very much. Encouraged by this, Jonny asked them to join him in the pool café where they could buy a warm drink and something to eat. Ivy was always ravenous after a swim so she accepted and Dot felt she should go along too as her sister appeared to be falling for Jonny's charm and might need rescuing if she became out of her depth – so to speak.

That day was the first of many when Ivy and Jonny would meet for a cup of tea and a slice or two of bread and jam or bread and dripping. Jonny insisted on paying the 1d per slice and Ivy let him as her new job wasn't paying enough to satisfy her post-swim hunger as well as her more frequent trips to the main pool so that she could make eyes at Jonny. Even to the naive Ivy, it was obvious that their relationship was blossoming into a romance and she was soon updating Dot with details of how Jonny had laughed at her jokes or tickled her as they drank their tea at the swimming baths. Prompting her to break into fits of giggles which caused her sparkling blue eyes to dance beneath her drying curls.

Although Ivy wasn't a particularly graceful dancer she sometimes accompanied Dot and her young man to a local dance hall. Chaperoned by her sister, Ivy would spend some carefree times with Jonny. His compliments and antics both flattered and amused her, a constant trigger for Ivy's giggles. Releasing the effervescence of her contagious laughter until she was fighting for breath. Dot loved to see her sister letting her hair down and having such fun. However, her affectionate sentiments didn't extend to Jonny. Smiling at the sight of Ivy smiling, Dot would dance with her beau until she was about to drop. They looked such a dapper couple as they glided and skipped across the floor, elegantly skating in perfect unison. But her own pleasure didn't deter Dot from keeping a keen eye on Jonny. There was a distinct mistrust which she just couldn't shake off.

Quizzing him about his job at the docks or his family, or some other inane subject, made little difference. In fact, the more time Dot spent interrogating him, the more she became suspicious of his intentions. In the absence of thumb screws, scrupulous examination of his behaviour would have to suffice.

No matter what Dot thought of him, Ivy was hook, line and sinker in love with him before the year was out. Jonny proclaimed he felt the same.

As a child, Ivy's mum had not been short of love for her children but praise and recognition came less frequently. Educational achievements were mentioned but not actively encouraged as the cost of sending a child to grammar school was out of reach for most people in the Ladbroke Grove area. Friends and neighbours thought it was "hoity toity" to stay on at school. Most would leave at fourteen years of age and, if lucky, jump straight into a job in a shop or factory. The Grammar School uniforms and books would have cost a small fortune and the rule in her family was "one and all", so nobody went – despite Ivy and her siblings possessing the acumen. Their intelligence didn't go wasted, however, as they were all destined for various fulfilling lives.

What Ivy would really have liked was a little more recognition for her swimming achievements. After all, she had won a trophy or two for her school over the years and hardly ever asked her parents for money. Dot, on the other hand, seemed to have a natural ability to draw out compliments from her parents. She was musical and much more vivacious than Ivy. Not that she was jealous of her because that would have been quite alien to her but she couldn't help wishing she had something to make her mum proud of. Something she would mention to neighbours on a wash day or to the woman who ran the little Italian ice cream parlour on the western side of Ladbroke Grove. The neighbourhood was less than salubrious and Ivy didn't particularly want to be the subject of idle gossip but she didn't want to be overlooked either. Just to hear her name spoken by her mother with words which friends or neighbours would share with positivity. Pride amongst the community. Acknowledgment.

There were many pleasurable times spent at home, however. The women would sit and knit various garments for the family and friends whilst a stew or soup bubbled away on the stove. Aromas vied for air space, above the chattering and laughter of Ivy and her family. It was often Ivy's infectious laugh which would follow the sharing of some wise womanly words, or jokes which were mainly at her expense. A day-dreaming Ivy would often drift off to wonder if the delicate cardigans and romper suits they created, were symbols of something stronger than all of the stitches of the wool. Intricate patterns of individual threads intertwining into a whole new, single and strong article. Loops of wool linking arms in solidarity. Representative of a confetti of skills combining to form something so beautiful that it gives warmth and comfort for years and generations to come. Encompassing the essence of a family which knows and shares love which is, in turn, to be shared in cascades. A fluid family.

These times were so precious to her and it was no surprise that this was to become an integral part of the times she would spend with the many women who were to join the family – even for many years beyond her passing. Treasured memories of treasured people; stored carefully in treasure boxes without locks. Kept safe by pinafores and clothes pegs until such times as they needed to be shared and aired.

It was during one of these daydreams, evoked by the way her mum looked lovingly at the latest matinee jacket, that Ivy exercised her imagination. How amazing it would feel, she imagined, to be put on a pedestal by her own Prince Charming, who would sweep her off her feet and treasure *her* forever. Casting herself as Scarlett O'Hara, she became submerged in her own romantic epic which told of love and loss, passion and promises and, of course, a little taste of tragedy. Her life would be a production which any drama teacher would surely be proud of, and which would sell out at the ABC within minutes. Find its' way into a novella or two.

So it was hardly surprising that she soon fell for the compliments and sweet nothings Jonny whispered to her as he walked her home from work most evenings. His charm and sophistication wasn't wasted on her, making Jonny feel good to boot. If nothing else, it massaged his ego. Was it so wrong to want a rosy future for herself, knowing that her mum relied on her wages every week and could hardly cope if Ivy moved out as a married woman? Did it make her selfish to want a wedding when they were still experiencing the austerity of the war? Could Jonny support her when they had a family of their own, in a house of their own? Could she really contemplate giving up her job at the accountants? After all, wasn't there a pot of gold at the end of every rainbow – enough to support a whole family?

Assuring herself that her future was in the capable hands of destiny, Ivy decided that she should firmly cast aside all of these doubts. Within a heartbeat, Ivy had accepted Jonny's proposal, which came the week before National Registration in September 1938.

The following spring, ever the blushing bride, Ivy stepped out of the church looking radiant and content as the new Mrs Freeman. As was the custom, due to the shortage of non-essential items in the war, Ivy wore an heirloom of a wedding gown (never to be referred as a hand-me-down), and a borrowed veil. Money was certainly scarce but there was an abundance of beautiful flowers brightening up the streets of London. Her ornate bouquet of deep red roses and dancing white gipsophelia seemed to cascade graciously to the floor, like the resting feathers of a peacock. Testament to Londoners tentatively transforming their yards and small allotments into radiant flower beds, providing a small income.

Due to her shortened leg nobody could "donate" any shoes so she had splashed out on some white court shoes in Portobello Road. They may have looked elegant and stylish but, way before any revelry and dancing was even suggested, the shoes had started to crush and cripple her weaker foot. Still, Ivy knew they would benefit somebody else one day soon.

Marriage plans had been made rather hastily and Ivy had been intent on giving up her job in order to look after her new husband. However, Jonny had other ideas which only made Dot dislike him further still. She had always seen him as a shirker with an aptitude for disappearing when strong hands were called for. He had a habit of disappearing on a regular basis, only engaging in boastful conversation before stepping outside for a smoke. Other people usually smoked indoors but Jonny used the need for a cigarette to escape more tight corners than Harry Houdini.

In contrast to Ivy's hopes of her own home, they had started their married life under the same roof as Dot and the rest of the family. Although Jonny paid his way, the house-keeping was at least second on his list of priorities when he opened is pay packet on a Friday night. With a pint of Fullers pale ale costing 4d per pint, Jonny seemed to have no trouble lining the pockets of the landlords in Ladbroke Grove and probably the whole of north Kensington. Dot often wondered if Jonny was trying to stock up on beer by increasing his consumption as they brought back rationing – he just didn't realise that he wasn't a camel. Or that the beer he drank only passed through him to contribute to the murkiness of the Thames.

For some reason, probably because she loved him so much, Ivy ignored the tittle tattle about him having a bit on the side and even told Dot to wash her mouth out when she said she thought it was true. Why didn't Dot simply learn to like him? She could play the piano by ear, having heard a tune only once, but struggled to read sheet music. Ergo, Dot struggled to read Jonny – or so Ivy thought!

3   IRIS- THE WOMAN

It wasn't clear to Iris just exactly when she had become a woman. Her childhood and teenage years had melded into one long journey of family life and working life, making it virtually impossible to separate the two. Of course, there were memories defining certain times and events and her memory was as sharp as a tack. However, try as she might, she had to accept the possibility that the young Iris had been a prototype for the wife and mother she so dearly wanted to be.

Dreams of creating her own little haven of domesticity, Iris was becoming more like her beloved mum every day. Helping to dress, wash and play with her younger siblings, often led her to view her school days as a kind of respite. There was no doubt that she loved each and every one of them and didn't resent for one moment, helping Ivy around the house. The intelligent Iris also enjoyed the social aspect of school as well as learning. Like her mother, she was a bright child, with a promising future. Excelling in maths, English and drama gave her teachers hope for Iris. If she had been afforded a place at Southall Grammar School. Unfortunately it wasn't to be. Like so many of her peers, the cost of sending a child to such as school was beyond their budget. Finances had been tight during both wars but, for her step-father Henry, it wasn't something he was prepared to change. There was also the added fact that Henry wasn't prepared to spend money on Iris when he could spend it on his own children. It caused quite a rift within the household and Iris came to accept the fact that she would forgo any more education – for the time being.

Her life wasn't all chores and childcare. There were certain perks to being the oldest one still living at home. Trying to make the best of a bad lot, Iris always jumped at the chance to go to the fish and chip shop on a Thursday. Of course, like everyone else in the house, she loved the little pieces of crispy batter which came with the chips, if she asked. But unlike the adults in the house, she blatantly detested the hard, grey pickled eggs which actually bounced when dropped on the floor (a secret experiment). Just the thought of pickled walnuts, swimming in vinegar flavoured with wally juice literally made her heave. Invariably, Henry only gave her enough money for half of the children to have supper as portions were ample enough for them to share. So, determined not to miss out, Iris would pick a little hole in the corner of the newspaper wrapper and pinch salty chips as she walked back home. The nearer she got to home, the soggier the chips became as they soaked up the malt vinegar, making it harder and harder for her to resist. Hungry adults are almost as hungry as children so nobody ever noticed. They just tucked into them with slices of bread and butter without any notion of how many chips were missing. Iris had noticed, but not mentioned, how the amount of chips which made it all the way home was becoming fewer and fewer. One day she might forfeit this treat. One day, she promised herself, she would have enough money to buy her whole family fish and chips. Maybe she would even resist the temptation to pinch some from the packet on the way home? Or maybe she wouldn't!

So, leaving school at the tender age of fifteen, Iris joined her friends and found herself working to contribute to the household bills. Whereas her mum had spent her spare money and energy on swimming, Iris developed a love of dancing. Together with her best friend Rosie, she would spend hours twisting and jiving to the latest rock n roll hits. Turning up the volume on the radio to the maximum, they were oblivious to the shouts from Rosie's mum to "keep it down". In truth, her mum loved the music too and occasionally she would dance to the same hits with Rosie's dad – when the opportunity arose. Being married to one of seven brothers meant there were plenty such opportunities. They didn't wait for a reason, they simply gathered in one or other's houses for a night of Woodbine and whiskey!

Iris' passion for dancing wasn't limited to whirling around in the dance halls to the beat of Bill Haley. A local dance troupe met every week in the Baptist Church hall, further along Western Road, where they now lived. This captured her attention and she soon enrolled in "Vera's Versatiles". Along with children ranging from five to fifteen years of age. Iris revelled in her tap dancing lessons. Miss Vera's sister kept a steady tempo on the piano, with tunes from the Big Screen they learned shuffles and hops; taps and slides; showing "teeth and eyes" as they swung their arms in perfect unison. Showing great promise for developing other children's skills, Iris sometimes taught the younger ones in exchange for her own lessons. One of Rosie's neighbours had been encouraged by her parents to take up tap dancing, as opposed to her first choice of ballet. Taking the tiny five-year-old by the hand as they walked the short distance to the Church, Iris would tell her about the annual concerts they put on and described the bright costumes they got to wear. Having huge identical ribbons in their neatly styled hair.   Dancing identical steps which made one expertly choreographed sound. Lights beaming from the ceiling to make their eyes sparkle. And people clapping and smiling in admiration as they take a bow. Making it sound quite magical came easy to Iris. Feeding the little one's imagination and curiosity was surely a quality she had inherited from her mum, maybe even when she had been the same tender age. Iris's calm approach had also proved to be invaluable when the first boy joined the troupe. He had badgered his father for ballet lessons too but it wasn't considered "suitable" for boys at that time. Enrolling his son in tap dancing lessons instead the only compromise. Surely, having a son clicking his heels on the Black and White Minstrel Show was far less embarrassing than seeing him in a tutu?

Not only did tap dancing keep her trim figure in shape but regular performances kept Iris busy, although not too busy to spend time with Rosie. They spent hours daydreaming about the latest singers, mainly Little Richard – one day to be ditched for the up-and-coming Cliff Richards. The girls both pinned their hopes on going to see either of them in a live concert one day. The chance of such big stars actually coming to Southall was out of the question but still they hoped. This didn't deter them from going into the listening booth in a record shop at The Green. Even such a tight space provided a dance floor for as long as the sales assistant would allow - albeit two feet square! Playing songs by Cliff, Marty Wilde, Bobby Vee and others heart-throbs made up for the times when they really did have to turn the volume down at home. Clad in bobby socks and flaring skirts, they would dress as if they were actually going to a live performance - wanting to be noticed in the crowds for their style and unfaltering renditions of every song.

When they weren't obsessing over the pop stars of the day, Iris and Rosie also spent a lot of time with Rosie's many cousins. They were never quite sure if having seven uncles (and their numerous children) to entertain them was blessing or bane but they were never short of company. Like Iris, Rosie had grown up in an ever-expanding family who never tired of celebrations and bustling gatherings. The majority of such events took place in Rosie's house and would end well after mid-night when the men were in the throes of a card game and the children were top and tail in bed. Muffled sounds of men making accusatory remarks of "cheat" or "I win" barely disturbed the children but they stayed awake, never the less, telling the most fantastic tales of ghosts and sharing fabricated secrets. Cousin Richard, however, seldom came to Rosie's without his parents and appeared to Iris to be either lonely or aloof. She wasn't sure which, but she often wished he would join her and Rosie from time to time.

It was becoming obvious to Rosie that Iris was as keen on Richard nearly as much as she was on pinching soggy chips. Or Little Richard. Maybe it was just that Iris saw them both as dreamboats who shared a name. Either way, Iris was literally pleading with her to invite him to join them more often. They had all spent time together but Richard preferred to spend time in his own house as opposed to going out to the cinema with everyone, or even just the Rec. The girls secretly decided that this was because Richard had everything he needed at home (or rather everything he wanted). They sometimes giggled at the way he appeared to be spoilt by his parents as he was an only child and they clearly doted on him in a way which their own parents couldn't afford to. It seemed to Iris that Richard must be lonely without the melee, dramas and traumas which livened up her home so she rarely envied him. There were two exceptions, however. One was the way Richard dressed in what looked like new clothes, in the latest fashion, but still remained unassuming. The other was that he probably had his own bedroom.

One Saturday afternoon, after much pleading from Iris, Rosie agreed to visit Richard in Dudley Road to ask if he wanted to join them for a bike ride to the park. It was hardly surprising when he declined the invitation but, much to Iris' delight, he asked them into his house instead. This was the first time Iris had been in his house or even in such close proximity of Richard and she found herself feeling awkward and embarrassingly self-conscious. Having a brother, Iris wasn't exactly a stranger to being in male company but not the company of such a dish.

Try as she might, Iris couldn't help but take an extra-long look at him as he talked to Rosie about things which didn't really interest her. It didn't occur to her that she was distracted by Richard's good looks and sophistication. Her own hair was dark and wavy but Richard's hair curled tightly around his neat ears and complimented his deep, dark brown eyes. Standing at approximately five feet nine inches, he wasn't the tall, dark and handsome man she had spent so many hours dreaming of but he certainly was handsome. It struck her as somewhat "grown up" that he should be dressed in a shirt, tie and braces when he hadn't any plans to go out. Whilst Rosie and Richard talked, Iris found herself drinking every aspect of his presence to the point where she was totally unaware of him including her in the conversation. His words washed over her and finally tuning back into the conversation only fuelled her crimson blushes.

If she had a response it alluded her and Iris was to be eternally grateful to Rosie for intervening when she did. Apparently they had arranged to take a picnic to the park over the other side of town and Rosie had volunteered Iris' sandwich making skills for the trip. Never before had Iris felt the pressure of preparing a picnic. It was, after all, to be eaten by, and in the presence of, the young man she was rapidly falling hopelessly in love with.

Trips to Southall and Fassnidge Parks were soon to become a regular thing for Iris and Richard. Rosie had grown tired of playing a wall-flower and they enjoyed each other's company more and more. It didn't really didn't matter to them that Iris needed to take her younger sister with them as Southall park had a small area which was laid out like a town, complete with white lines in the road and the black and white stripes of the newly introduced zebra crossing. Borrowing the pedal cars and child-size bicycles was a favourite for all of them and they spent many hours trying to teach Iris' sister how to balance and steer the bicycle all at once.

They had even started to go on outings with Richard's parents as it provided the opportunity to spend more time together. To Iris, the main blot on the landscape was when she had to accompany her own family on holidays to Butlin's or some other seaside town which seemed to be at the end of the world. It was during these periods of separation that their love deepened and they came to dream and plan their future together. Dreams which were recorded on tear-stained paper for posterity. They would have three children, a house in the country and holidays with their own family to far-reaching places such as Cornwall or even across the channel to exotic places made for film-stars (and her family). Experiencing long days out on Richard's motorbike with friends, or bus rides into London (sometimes with one of Iris' younger siblings) only reinforced their wanderlust and dreams. They say love has no bounds and this was certainly the case for Iris Freeman and Richard Lord.

Although they talked – frequently – about their future, it came as quite a surprise when Iris found herself pregnant at the tender age of seventeen. Her mum had certainly told her all about "the birds and the bees", or rather she had given her a small handbook which was printed by some kind of government body, and told to read it. Whilst it was informative enough it didn't offer as much information or facts as Iris had gleaned from living in such a large family. Neither did it give any tips on how to tell her parents the situation or tell Richard's parents she was "in the family way". Maybe it helped that Ivy was also expecting another baby that year, although Iris wouldn't be at hand to help with changing nappies and the likes. In reality, the task of sharing their news was received better than they expected.

As predicted, Maud and Edward were not best pleased and seem to believe that Richard would *need* to "make an honest woman of her" rather than *love* to. Discussions were instantly had about the practicalities and logistics of welcoming Iris into the family. Edward industriously set about sprucing up the likes of a cot and high chair. Maud set about knitting matinee coats, embroidering tiny nightgowns fashioned from white sheets and fastened with pearly buttons from her sewing box. It might not have been obvious to the average onlooker, but Maud indulged herself in the surrogate nesting for her first grandchild.

In stark contrast, Ivy was so pleased for them. Now her own daughter was to be swept off her feet by her own Knight in shining armour – or at least a Lord in long trousers. Of course, she was shocked and when the four parents all met to discuss wedding and living arrangements, Ivy was more than a little protective over Iris. A hint of judgement of any of her precious children brought a ferocity to her beyond belief. However, Maud and Edward welcomed the fusion of families and obviously loved Iris. And so, her defence mechanism remained charged but latent, never extinguished for one single moment. All three women instantly started to weave their bond with knitting needles and three ply wool. Four ply would come later.

The obstacle of sharing their news was to be many they would face along their journey together. However, they couldn't have been more certain when they made their vows to each other in the summer of 1958. It was agreed that Iris wouldn't wear a long, ostentatious gown as they were to marry in a Registry Office. However, sporting a new, figure hugging suit, Iris looked every part the blushing bride and believed that she could never be happier than she was that day in June. Nestled in her small bouquet was the tiniest bud. One that would, in Iris' wise young mind, grow and blossom as a symbol of the rosy future she prayed for. Thorns might lay behind the leaves but the sheer beauty of the bloom would keep them securely in shadow. Contained but not concealed.

Four Leaf Clover

4   MAUD – THE MOTHER

Richard Archibald Lord came kicking and screaming into this world within the confines of the delivery suite at St Mary's Hospital, Paddington. This wasn't the nearest hospital from their home in Dudley Road but, due to her tiny stature Maud had needed "special help" with delivering her baby. Visiting times were strict during her confinement and the Matron would not hesitate to ring the little brass bell on her workstation if she decided there were too many women having visitors or if they dared to even contemplate overstaying visiting time. Edward was introduced to his son when he was three days old. An exhausted Maud had not been well enough for visitors, the doctors said, and Edward duly waited and treasured the peek he had of the little blond bundle pointed out to him in the nursery. The sound of wailing muffled behind the glass of the nursery window. Worried about not having had much experience with babies was a feeling which dissipated as he proudly looked down. This was *his* son and he had married the perfect woman as a mother for him. Not only was she beautiful and kind but, after all, she was more than qualified to nurture and treasure their son – with more love than she had ever afforded him, or any of the men who had been raised in her care. Whilst the fact that their precious child was another male in the family didn't go unnoticed by Edward, it seemed to him that Richard Archibald was truly a gift from God.

To continue her confinement, Maud arrived home in the ambulance, as was the way in 1938. The new parents proudly introduced Richard to his grandfather and a string of relatives waiting to meet the latest addition to the ever-growing family. More than once, Maud heard someone say "maybe the next one will be a girl" as if Richard was somehow a substitute baby. Do-gooders were prone to saying "look at his lovely blond curls, dress him in blue in case people think he's a girl"! The tittle tattlers couldn't have been more wrong. Maud and Edward were such devoted parents who doted on their son every waking moment. Even if the baby had been a girl, she wouldn't have been loved any more or even spoilt quite as much as Richard was to be. Sunday school readings had ingrained the proverb "spare the rod and spoil the child" into her memory. That was the day she threw away the rod.

As the joyful months rolled by, Maud really relaxed into motherhood and enjoyed walking out with the baby to the Manor Grounds. Pushing him in his black coach-built pram, complete with a Broderie-Anglaise sun canopy which was lined with dark green cotton. It was believed that green was a soothing colour, hence sun shades and theatre scrubs were made in various green hues and Maud insisted on doing as the professionals advised (when it suited). There were rules and guidance which she chose to ignore, such as not rubbing whisky on the painful gums of a teething baby. Her father and grandfather might not have been particularly knowledgeable of the nursing practices of a new-born but they had both resorted to using this form of anaesthetic when left holding a screaming boy.

Managing to keep Richard warm in his early months, as he was an autumn baby, was difficult. Coal fires and bed warming pans proved to be a saving grace, together with the multitude of matinee jackets, booties and romper suits Maud fashioned. They were all lovingly knitted with brand new wool but any old pillow cases or sheets made for perfect gowns and nightdresses. Her beautiful son was swaddled in bed linen which she had made herself, embroidering intricate patterns in the corners as well as being snuggled in his pram under one of the many blankets she had crocheted for him. The traumatic birth hadn't quite been relegated to a distant memory yet. Maud became weary of women who said how amazing it was that the pains of childbirth melted away with your heart as soon as the baby was born. It was true that she instantly loved her new-born son, but the emotional (if not the physical) scars still had some healing to do. This was something which played on her mind more frequently than Maud would have liked, appreciating just how brave her mother must have been to bare nine babies.

At the turn of the century it was custom for women to deliver their babies at home and her mother had been no different. Although Maud couldn't imagine how she had coped in the tiny Victorian home, her respect for her mother multiplied ten-fold as she became a mother herself. Many a time, Maud would find herself wondering just how her mother managed with the demands of a new-born; how she learnt the meaning of so many individual cries he would emit; who had been there for her when she was faced with something as alien as weaning the baby from the breast – without making him a soap sandwich!

The love she had for her son was all consuming and, at times, overwhelming, which she relished and quickly found herself behaving a little rebellious as she ignored the midwife's rules and spent as much time cuddling and cajoling Richard as she wanted. She hadn't laboured in vain – to follow rules which were better suited to a mother with a disability and deny her baby the softness of his mother's breast when he wanted it. She knew, without a shadow of a doubt, that this was something beautiful which only she could give him. It was both a need and a privilege.

In addition to devoting herself to her new family, and her father, Maud was finally reaping the benefits of married life. Not only did she feel she had a better social standing, sporting a wedding band, but they also had the unexpected addition of extra income for the household. Edward was in a steady and skilled job in the wood yard in Dawley Road which paid well and afforded them real luxuries such as the occasional tipple of peach wine and extra film for Edward's Box Brownie camera. Maud liked to think that his photographic skills were his way of capturing memories for prosperity. Edward seldom expressed his emotions and yet his photographs, especially the ones of Richard, seemed to touch the hearts of so many. They had even converted some of the attic space into a dark room so that he could take as many photographs of Richard as he wanted without the added processing costs. Even though the finished photographs were in black and white, Edward always managed to adjust the exposure exactly right so as to highlight just how blond Richard's curls were in stark contrast to his deep, dark brown eyes. The care he took over his photographs, processed under the low ceilings of the attic, was testament the devotion he showed his new family and their families to come.

Being the "most photographed baby in Southall" meant Richard was always well turned out in various outfits which weren't exactly complimented by the bulging Zorbit terry towelling nappies he wore underneath. Such was their desire to give Richard everything he needed (and more) that Maud bought him a solid gold brooch which had the word "baby" written across a delicate mother-of-pearl background. The blatant extravagance was so out of character for her, and the butt of some teasing from her brothers who said that she should have remembered the baby's name by now – Richard was ten months old after all. Maud had retorted that she labelled everything from batteries to boot polish to see how long it was lasting; and why should her son be any different? The latter part being somewhat of a fib – Richard *was* different and more special than any baby ever born into the World. As was evident by the fact that his "label" wasn't hand written on a piece of masking tape!

Maud's contentment with her life was about to shatter into a million pieces, along with that of the rest of Europe, as Churchill announced that they were at war with Germany. Within a few short weeks Maud's life had been torn from the bliss of parenthood to the bedlam and mayhem of preparing for her husband to go to war. Hadn't she been used to being the strong and resilient one? Hadn't years of organising, budgeting, scrimping and saving taught her how to manage in times of trouble? The answers were always "yes" but that didn't mean she would cope with this situation. And it didn't mean she could cope without the love and protection of having Edward by her side. If Maud were the cursing type she would have said a few strong words to Churchill, Adolf Hitler and the War Office all at once. As she wasn't such a brazen hussy Maud would just have to accept that it was her duty to keep the home running and Richard safe whilst Edward joined the Royal Artillery and fought for King and country. Being patriotic was far from her mind. Maud could have shed a torrent of tears for every man who trod the fields of Europe before Edward and an ocean for those who were to follow him. Great comfort was to be had in the belief that it was all going to be over by Christmas.

The air raids came thick and fast, unrelenting as Richard celebrated his first birthday with an outing to the Anderson shelter at the bottom of their garden. It was there that Maud felt at her lowest ebb and most vulnerable. Sitting in the dark, cuddling Richard in an attempt to alleviate some of his distress as the bombs screeched down, Maud let her tears fall freely on more than one occasion. Tears which may have been absorbed by the shawl in which Richard was cocooned, but were plenty enough to sit on the lenses of her glasses. Reflecting the chaos raging all around which rolled away with every attempt to capture and remove them. Tears held in until drawn out by the solitude of an air raid with an unquenchable thirst. As if the falling tears of mothers was their defence against the raging fires of war. A war effort.

All kinds of sins and secrets were occurring under the cover of darkness and Maud felt that it was extremely self-indulgent and almost sinful to shed tears when she was "lucky" enough to have her own shelter. Mrs Sparks, at number 66, had been invited into the shelter with her little boy too but she mostly declined as she didn't want to impose. Maybe she also gave in to the waves of emotion which were held behind a teetering sea wall, only to come crashing down with every German bomb. Even though Maud had become quite friendly with her neighbour it had crossed her mind that this was the reason for her staying in her house during the air raids. Each woman saving herself the shame of showing any self-pity, attached to the guilt they felt with each tear they shed. Women filled with embarrassment of experiencing emotions felt by mothers and wives nationwide. Divided by the very thing which, in the light of day, united them.

With war came ration books – again. It seemed to Maud that her world was turning a full circle as she was faced with the stark reality of being left to "make do and mend". Yet again, it seemed to Maud, the men in the world had taken it upon themselves to try and bring some order to a quite disorderly situation. Sanity trying to take control in an insane World. Replacing the fear of battle with the equally tangible fear of the inevitable losses in battle. Men had started this war and men would have to end it. Men would have to fix it if it was to be in any fit state for Richard to inherit. Men would have to ensure the legacy her son would receive would be of a free, prosperous and plentiful future. The women would just have to make sure the men did what was needed! Maud was under no illusion about her real role in the war effort. She was more than prepared to roll her sleeves up and attack whatever strife she encountered. For it wasn't her country she was fighting for – it was her son's survival and his future. What did they call it? A green and pleasant land? There wasn't much greenery in Southall, even in 1940, but Maud knew it was out there somewhere and she became fiercely determined to show it to her son as soon as the war was over.

The next six years were to bring unimaginable pain and loss for so many. Whilst Maud poured all of her attention and energy into keeping the house and family safe she was acutely aware that Edward was quite literally battling through his time in the Army. Contact between them had been scarce and, although Edward was not accustomed to writing letters, Maud still wrote to him and gleaned as much information as she could from other soldier's wives. Sending letters which might be lost in transit seemed never-ending but never futile. With the slightest possibility of her letters reaching her husband and giving him a glimmer of hope for a future with Richard and her, the letters became an essential part of Maud's' week. She applied almost as much determination when refusing to think of her own brothers so far away from home too. Knowing she had one baby in her arms was far removed from feeling like she had so many children who had donned a uniform to perform duties beyond their imaginations. But there was no mistaking the reality of the end of the war.

On 2nd September 1945 the news came that Germany had surrendered. It was almost more than Maud could comprehend. Not only had she survived the air raids over West London, but she had also managed to undertake some essential tasks of parenthood by enrolling Richard into Featherstone Road Infant's School at the top of the road and keeping the house as spick and span. A home she thought Edward would want to find on his return. After all, wasn't he fighting for their future? As far as Maud could see, the future had already started. They stood as man and wife at the altar and they would stand as man and wife again – with Richard binding them even closer together. A perennial bond, stronger than the gold wedding band and three shining diamonds which still adorned her tiny hands.

It was winter before Edward came home. A very cold and unforgiving winter with biting winds and snow blizzards sweeping across the south. No serge great-coat could keep out the iciness of the air and protect the skin from Jack Frost's assaults on the faces of soldiers, returning from the trenches. Buckles on sleeves may have prevented water from running down the arms when using binoculars in the rain, but they did little to shield their hands from the snowdrifts shrouding the country for which they had so heroically fought. Edward, like so many of his comrades, had endured the most unimaginable atrocities during the past few years. The very least of all being exposed to the extreme elements, while trying to overcome sleep and warmth deprivation. Forming friendships which were to last a lifetime – that lifetime all too often being the few short weeks or months they spent together in battle, their parting being death or de-mob.

Yet he had never stopped thinking of his treasured wife and son he had been so devastated to leave behind. The image of Maud rushing into his arms with Richard on her hip is what kept Edward pressing forward. Whilst he knew that Richard was growing, he treasured the memory of the chubby toddler whom he had kissed goodbye.

Sleeping in army cots which were far removed from the bed at home which accommodated his tall frame. Sleeping, whenever he was told to, in a bed which held a chill no bed-warmer could touch. Sleeping alone with the battle sounds raging in his ears when all he dreamed of was the wailing sound of his boy. Explosions so loud they shook him to his very soul, threatening to shatter the love in his heart into a million shards of unyielding steel. Flashes of spiked glass which reflected scenes of long-lost security, and were fuddled with brief glimpses of home bound roads. Leading to the freedom from war he craved, along unrecognisable paths.

Then why, it seemed to Maud, had his home-coming been so stilted? Europe was alive with a sense of rebirth. The giddy frenzy of celebrations reverberated across the country. Bomb fires were replaced with bonfires. Lightbulbs burst out of hibernation. Maud wanted Edward to embrace her as neighbours and strangers had embraced her during the many impromptu street parties. To hold her as if he would never leave her again but something told her that he just couldn't do it. Maybe her love and warmth would help to defrost the iciness he bought back with him from the war? Maybe the spring sunshine would bring a glow back to his ruddy cheeks? Maybe the sea breeze in the summer would blow away his trench coat which played as much a part of keeping the cold out as keeping it trapped in?

Their future had continued during the war years, as she believed, but Maud was no fool and she rolled up her sleeves to ensure her family enjoyed the future she had been striving for. If it was to be half as blissful as the first few years of their marriage, some serious effort was needed to ensure the future which Edward had been striving for. There was no better time to make this effort than during the August factory shut downs.

As was the fashion, or necessity, Maud prepared and packed the trunks for a summer holiday with her two favourite "boys". Edward hadn't learned to drive so, without a car, Maud's only option was to send their luggage on ahead a week before they travelled. It would be waiting at the guest house in Birchington-on-Sea upon their arrival, as if by magic. This was also something which Edward appreciated as it was quite an arduous train journey _ taking them through the heart London before rattling along the tracks and out into the country – the green and pleasant land.

On their arrival an excited Richard pleaded with Maud to take him to the beach but it was Edward who strolled down to the sand with their son. It was Edward who bought Richard his very own cricket set with bails, a wicket and a red leather ball. It was also Edward who quietly rose to the challenge of teaching Richard how to actually play cricket with only two in the team. It was no surprise then, that Richard had the notion that he would either be the batsman or the bowler – in every game he came to play. Either way, he was the most important player on the field (or beach). To his own shouts of "a perfect arm ball from Lord" and "just watch him bowl his signature bouncer" Richard revelled in being the commentator as well! A quiet, rueful smile also spread across Edward's face as he heard his son apply some rhyming slang to his narrative. It was true that the beach did lend itself to a particular bowling style was, in fact, "a Bunsen" but it came as a surprise that Richard knew this phrase at all. Cockney rhyming slang didn't feature much, if at all, in the time-tables of Featherstone Road Infant School!

As usual, Maud busied herself with unpacking their luggage, disappointed whenever she discovered a crease or two in one of Edward's shirts. Having spent her formative years ensuring the men in the family were well turned out, she certainly knew how to fold and maintain intentional sharp creases. Even the sea breeze couldn't quite blow away her irritation but her mood did change tack as she unpacked for her son. Maud smiled to into the sparsely decorated room as she placed Richard's swimming shorts into the drawer. As a surprise, Maud had lovingly crocheted them, in a very fetching mustard yellow wool. She had contemplated buying either a pillar box red or any colour which reflected the fun and excitement they would have on their holiday. Instead, the yellow had caught her eye as a cheerful colour. Despite approaching his seventh birthday, Maud knew he would be thrilled with them. After all, they were not second-hand and nobody else on the beach would have a pair the same as him. Ironically, the truth of this point would prove to be the catalyst of events which saw Richard staggering from the surf, desperately clutching his shorts with the most unamused expression on his face. Whilst it had been fun to jump in the waves (he would never be a strong swimmer) it most certainly wasn't fun to discover your home-made, newly crocheted swimming shorts simply absorbed the sea water to the extent where they became really, really heavy. Heavy enough to fall down!

Richard's embarrassment was hardly spared as Mr & Mrs Edward Lord insisted on visiting the same guest house for all future holidays. For many years to come, Richard remained fearful of meeting anyone who had been witness to his moment of horror. As a result, Richard showed a determination he inherited from his mother when refusing to wear anything crocheted on the beach! Determination gave way to resolve when he was presented a pair of trunks which, although they were shop bought, his older cousins no longer needed. Third hand was just perfect to him.

Every year they had tea in the café on the corner, serving the most spectacular ice cream sundaes to children who ate every scrap of their fish and chips first. Maud was always had fond memories of the first such occasion when she had insisted on eating inside the café as opposed to by the seafront. There were few demands she made, especially when spending hard earned money. However, could not be persuaded to eat the meal out of the paper, in public, with her fingers. In Maud's adamant mind, such behaviour was reserved – yet again – for those less well-mannered than herself. With the exception of the occasional ham sandwich wrapped in greaseproof paper, Maud would never partake in such a practice. After all, how would she "save some for Miss Manners"?

This was something which Richard both respected and resented in equal measures. As an adult, he was to become fond of eating his supper on the beach, as the seagulls scavenged around him. Until, that was, he was deprived of his cod by an extremely large and aggressive bird as it swooped down – Spitfire style – and whipped it from his clutches.

Eating habits aside, it wasn't until Richard reached his teenage years that they felt they may have exhausted what the Birchington area had to offer and they took to spending holidays in Somerset. Naturally, with such a big family, there were opportunities to stay with relatives at coastal towns in Essex, and other accessible places. By this time Maud had resisted the temptation to crochet Richard another pair of swimming trunks, as he had inevitably outgrown the original pair. Needless to say this was much to the relief of Richard and certainly saved the embarrassment of other holiday makers. She conceded that it really was time to buy some new ones, frivolous or not.

As he grew and matured, Maud continued to overindulge Richard, as he was indeed their only child. Not only did he have fabulous wooden toys made by Edward, the attention of his grandfather and uncles – with their respective wives and children as well as his treasured cricket bat. Soon this would prove to be more of a blight than a benefit. Richard's parents had tried hard to instil patience, understanding and the ability to accept defeat as virtues. However, one day after their first trip to Birchington-on-Sea, Richard had asked if he could play cricket with some other boys on the grassy area at the end of the road. Having been given permission by Maud, Richard set off with his cricket set under his arm. Proudly sporting the bat, Richard announced that he would bat first *and* be the Captain of both sides. David Sparks was appointed as the bowler *and* umpire as he was the boy who Richard trusted the most. Not wanting to argue, the other boys settled into roles of wicket keepers and fielders. The game progressed well for some time with Richard and David scoring the most runs. There were certainly many opportunities for a dead ball – awarding five penalty runs for Richard –which David duly awarded him. There were also other "rules" which Richard introduced, insisting they were mainly used in test cricket, which the others couldn't be expected to know! However, when it began to look like the tables were strangely turning, Richard promptly announced that the game was over and he sauntered the hundred yards back to his house with David in tow – taking the leather ball with him.

They say "Pride comes before a fall" and Maud was certainly proud of her son and all he had achieved. Richard had shown an aptitude for designing and creating various gifts and gadgets but, more importantly, he had earned a place at the local Grammar School. The uniform and extra-curricular activities would mean an added expense but she no longer had to scrimp and save the way she had when she was first married. They even had a television which neighbours crowded round to see important broadcasts like the King's funeral and the young Princess Elizabeth at her investiture.

Edward had still not learned to drive, however, and it would have been quite something to have the use of a car. Occasionally he would get dropped off at the end of the day by a colleague driving a blue truck. The back of it was over-flowing with planks of wood, intensifying the sweet aroma of fresh wood shavings which wafted into the house when Edward arrived home. Maud might not have appreciated the sawdust which he invariably trod into the hall carpet but she let the smell of the freshly sawn wood soothe her into familiar wedded bliss, thankful that Edward had come home safely for another day at least. The wood yard where he worked was far from the dangers and threats of the trenches, but Maud never really erased the memories of being separated from him which haunted her. Maud hoped that, one day, Edward would return from work with his painful memories having been chiselled into a distant past and left on the ground like the wood-shavings. Believing that they shouldn't be swept away completely, as this would mean the path of sacrifice made by men in the war wouldn't be there for men to follow in peace

38

5   IVY – THE MOTHER

With World War 2 breaking out in Europe, and London experiencing bombing like never before, it had hardly been an ideal time to find herself pregnant. Jonny had been more than disappointed to say the least as Ivy completed her last day at work and, with her belly swelling daily, settled into a very short period of nesting. The household was becoming busier, with all of them under one roof and Dot had still not warmed to her brother-in-law so tensions were running high when Ivy went into hospital for her confinement. As Jonny walked away from her, at the door, she found herself craving the chaos of home which seemed a lifetime away from the solitude and isolation of the delivery suite.

"Bombed last night, bombed the night before…" had become Ivy's mantra as she battled with surging contractions and the accompanying exhaustion of labour. Her mum had told her that there's no pain like giving birth and she had been right. So she must have been right when she said the pain is worth it when you hold your little bundle for the first time, Ivy hoped. Her mum didn't tell her, however, was that the pain in her womb would give way to a pain in her heart as her chest filled with pride and unconditional love for her child. A pain she would willingly endure for each and every baby she bore.

Little Iris May Freeman arrived in the midst of an air raid which meant that Ivy hadn't been in the safety of the underground tube station with her family at the time. Until then, there had been bombs dropping so regularly that she had begun to think that she would give birth to her baby in a shelter or on a bomb site. Rather naively, Ivy had the vision of her baby "falling" from her like a doodle bug. Of women's cries resounding around the hospital, in competition with air raid sirens. The screeching and wailing serenading their babes into the World. A fanfare matched by no other as a new generation was born to a London adorned with white towelling nappies – instead of the Union Jack. Some babies had even been pushed up the chimney during the blitz to keep them in the strongest part of the house so Ivy was grateful that her baby was swaddled in clean white sheets from the start of her precious life. To some, the hungry wailing of the new-born babies could also be confused with the similar sound of the claxon sounding. But Ivy knew her daughter's cry as soon as she met her.

For a young woman of just twenty one she had bonded instantly with her baby girl and showered her with cuddles and kisses. Even though it was believed to be "bad for baby" as it was making a rod for her own back, Ivy just couldn't resist drinking in every inch of the new-born's very being. When Iris was wheeled to the nursery with the other babies, Ivy would swear that she felt the air leaving her own lungs so as to ensure her daughter had enough breath to last the hours without her. When the strict and starched nurses brought her back, Ivy nursed her daughter until her little belly was full. With a tenderness borne of devotion, it was Ivy's turn to gently place her swaddled baby on a pedestal, stepping aside to make way.

As Ivy continued to be totally absorbed with motherhood she didn't pay too much attention to the snipes and quips which came from Dot (and now her own fiancée). Whilst contentment never lingered beyond the hours spent nursing Iris, she felt it all the same. Berated by some for indulging in pleasures brought by the unique smells and softness of a baby's skin. Such judgments and criticism was quickly cast aside, but the strain of raising Iris without Jonny around was starting to show. He had been smitten when he first laid eyes on Iris and appeared to play it cool whenever someone mentioned what an adorable baby she was. Ivy was astute enough to sense that there was a special father–daughter bond forming between Jonny and Iris. On more than one occasion, she had seen snippets of the tenderness he felt towards this beautiful baby girl. Glimpses of the softness of Iris's cheeks reflected in his eyes, as he, in turn, gazed in awe at the stunning blue eyes she had inherited from her mother.

Those were the times Ivy preferred to remember and savour. In reality, had she dared to invite other memories into her mind, her contentment was evaporating before her lavender eyes.

Men generally had little involvement in the practical aspects of raising a child, and Jonny was no different. When asked to hold Iris for a moment, or to pass a pin as Ivy balanced her baby on her lap for yet another nappy change, Jonny "needed" a cigarette. Many a night, Ivy would roll across their bed to a waking baby, and Jonny would roll out of bed to a smoke. Silently returning to the sanctuary of the covers, perched on the respective edges of the mattress in wait for the next feed. Dawn brought bright new light, which served to illuminate all routes to dusk. Ivy would never know if it was her that he was running away from one Friday night in May or the notion of being called up for National Service. Either way, life after 1940 would never be the same for her.

Sheer grit and determination were qualities which Ivy possessed in abundance and applied to her every-day life as she found herself a lone parent during a second war. In an amazing twist of fate her job was still available due to the fact that her replacement had been called up to join the Army. So, when she needed to provide for Iris a doting grandmother had readily agreed to look after the baby whilst she worked. By then, even Dot had stopped having digs about what a lay-about Jonny had proven to be. There had been no word from him directly but Ivy had seen his sister and it was widely speculated that Jonny had fled to Jersey in an attempt to avoid Conscription. Dot's only comment was "it's a shame he doesn't speak German".

Ivy was torn between an overwhelming sense of rejection and a heart breaking sadness that Iris was going to miss out on seeing her own dad as she grew up. Yet, try as she might, Ivy couldn't bring herself to hate him. He may well have chosen a life without her and Iris, but she knew he had loved her when they married and she knew he loved their beautiful baby girl. Although he had chosen a life without them, Jonny's sister had come to Ivy's work one day and handed her a tiny box with a gold cross inside. It was the first and only gift he was to give Iris and she would wear and treasure it for her entire life.

Whilst Ivy fully respected and loved her mum, somewhere along the line she had decided that she would be different with her own child. Maybe it was partly because material items were either luxuries or carefully rationed so Ivy gave the very thing which she knew she couldn't buy on the black market ... Love. Her daughter made this quite easy as she was a contented child, entertaining and melting the hearts of all those who met her. This included all of her relatives and even the lodgers Dot and her new husband had taken in when they got married – which was naturally a more lavish affair than Ivy's wedding.

However, no matter how much love and attention Ivy had bestowed upon her nothing could alleviate the trauma of the continuous air-raids. Unrelentingly screeching from the skies towards London, nobody could prepare them for the magnitude of the explosions. Ivy joined others in the underground stations. Here it was possible for families to huddle together for support. Used previously during the First World War, the tunnels provided shelter for Londoners as well as for covert munitions productions.

As the debris from buildings which had been raised to the ground was blown down onto the station platforms, Ivy tried desperately to pacify a distraught Iris. Gas leaks and fires were dotted across the city as the families waited with baited breath were given the "all clear" by the Wardens. For many, returning home wasn't an option as their home was now no more than a pile of dusty bricks. Ivy shuddered to think that her house could be next. There was to be no escape from the trauma of hearing about friends and neighbours who perished in the crush at Bethnal Green in March. Visions of so many people, seeking refuge from the relentless bombing, trapped in the very place they were led to believe was safe. As safe as houses? She could only pray for them, and count her blessings that she had been able to keep Iris safe until her second birthday, at least.

Children from the capital were being evacuated into various places around the country but, despite Ivy knowing it was safer for her daughter to travel out of London, the sheer thought of being separated from her just crushed her. What had her mum said to her when she was struggling to find resilience she needed? "Nobody ever got thin from worrying about being fat. Nobody ever got tall by worrying about being small". No amount of crying was going to protect Iris so Ivy reluctantly accepted a placement in the place where they would be safe together.

Air raids were comparatively unheard of in the Welsh valleys as the Messerschmitt's focused their attention and bombs on coastal towns. Children were being evacuated as far away from the channel as possible. Germany may have the resources to fight Spitfires in the air. They even had the technology to carry bombs which could obliterate whole communities. What they lacked was the capacity for enough fuel to fly their bombers across the channel, deep into rural England, and return back to occupied France. Ivy struggled to seek solace in this but, if she was to survive in a country so desperately under threat, she would take heed of the government advice and leave. The skyline of London she awoke to in the mornings was far removed from that which she knew and loved. This was no longer a place in which Ivy could build happy memories for Iris. Maybe Wales would be the place for them to create wonderful, indelible memories together. Built on foundations of fresh green grass, love and togetherness. Nourished by pure country air and skies heavy with a blitz of refreshing rain. The two of them would have an adventure and grow strong and healthy together.

In reality, the family they were placed with didn't have an Anderson shelter, most villagers had Morrison shelters in their homes which provided them with a sturdy "table" as well as something to hide under. Seen as a small mercy, Ivy accepted that the coastal air raids in Cardiff and Swansea were probably going to be less of a danger to her precious daughter. So she packed their belongings – not forgetting Iris' tiny gold cross.

Although Ivy had spent short holidays in Kent, between the wars, she hadn't travelled far from home before. Any trepidation she had soon evaporated when the train started to trundle along the track out into the open fields and palpable fresh country air filled her lungs. Iris' cheeks glowed brighter with every passing station. Whilst she marvelled at her daughter's excitement as virtually everything she saw, Ivy wasn't yet ready to relax but, as the knots in her stomach turned to butterflies she dared to indulge in a tiny weeny fantasy. No longer cast as Scarlett O'Hara, Ivy was to play the leading role in the most wondrous story any little girl would want to hear. It was to be a magical fairy-tale of two lady spiders, spinning a web stronger than anyone could imagine. Fine threads of gossamer deemed it invisible to the naked eye but nothing in the world, let alone their Kingdom, could break through. For there were two magic ingredients woven carefully within the spirals. Faith and Love. A mother's love.

It was a long, long journey but one which took them to the heart of a village which captured an amazing sense of peace and tranquillity. Grass greener than they had ever seen, shaded by trees so tall that Ivy told Iris that they reached so high they could touch heaven. With strong roots nourished by the (frequent) rain, majestic branches and leaves served as an unbreakable bridge between Heaven and Earth. The tall mountains were really sentry boxes for the Queen's guards - giving the protection they needed from the ill winds which sneaked across the seas. There was no doubt in Ivy's mind, and her growing daughter's, that such beauty and magnificence could only be the work of God. They had faith.

The two of them soon settled into life in the breath-taking beautiful area of Mountain Ash. Ivy revelled in the opportunity to spend more time with Iris when she had finished a variety of chores, as her contribution to the war effort. There was no distractions from bombings, office work, pacifying neighbours who had lost their homes to the blitz or even queueing for food. Eggs were available more freely in the country and Ivy found it heart-warming to see how the neighbours "traded" carrots for eggs and eggs for potatoes. The whole sense of a community reminded her of the spirit which saw Londoners bond in unity. Somehow this surprised her. Her own mum would pass down outgrown clothes to friends and neighbours but this wasn't necessarily in exchange for specific belongings. It was just the London way.

Ivy's eyes were now opened to the Mountain Ash way too. Ivy was more than pleased to show off her culinary skills by cooking for her host family. Even with barely enough rationed meat to feed a sparrow (or the owls which called out into the dark nights), Ivy's mum had taught her how to cook the most delicious stews and suet puddings. None of the dishes required following a recipe which made it easier to be creative with what-ever ingredients were at hand. She could rustle up some wholesome bread pudding when she could get her hands on a cup of currants. Morsels of bacon, mixed with onions and any vegetable available, became encased in a thick steamed suet pudding - an amazing bacon roll. Suet saved the day. The family had hardly been starving in London but cooking with powdered egg and the tiniest rations had meant they had to make do with much cheaper cuts – or scraps – of meat.

In Wales many of the houses had enough of a garden to grow vegetables and it was rumoured that houses in London had little yards and grew only carrots - which was turning the children orange. Thankfully, Iris had her mother's natural tendency to absorb the suns' rays and she seemed to have a healthy glow to her small cheeks. Also, like her mother, Iris had the most piercing blue eyes and people in the street would often comment on how startlingly beautiful they were. The local people in the village loved her instantly, with her infectious smile and the tinkle of her laugh. Her little face almost danced when she giggled. A dance which would, one day, accompany the song of her life, sang like a lullaby to the babes who were blessed to find themselves in the folds of her own warmth and love. A mother's love.

Ivy still sported the suntan on her smooth skin when she returned to London as the war ended. This time things were not as easy as they had seemed in the past. Was it true that future generations were to fall on harder times as the years went by? She hoped not because life in post-war London was even more difficult than before. Ivy refused to believe this as it suggested that all the losses, fear, and devastation of the war years had been a waste. It was up to her to somehow make Iris's future as rosy as she could.

Landmarks were disappearing fast in London, the Germans targeting them with relentless precision. Ivy knew that, one day, she would return to Kensington and find homes had been obliterated. Schools and shops mere piles of red dusty bricks. Unexploded bombs in furrows of green parkland. It seemed to her that the Germans had laid a huge, dark shroud over her home town. In the melee of war they may have thrown Europe into periods of darkness, but she and Iris had enough light in their hearts and sparkling eyes to cast long shadows over the destruction.

There was no way for Ivy to support herself or her daughter, even though they were living back with her mum and other relatives. The Blitz had taken its' toll on Ladbroke Grove and people were moving further outside London wherever possible. Assistance was available for families who wanted a fresh start and many of Ivy's friends took advantage of this. Cousins moved to the suburbs, attracted by the brand new homes in brand new estates. By pastures new –in Slough. Schools and shops, pubs and picture houses, all for the people known as the London overspill. For Ivy, the family bonds were too strong and she couldn't imagine being separated from her loved ones all over again. Being a single parent was proving to be virtually insurmountable, even with the emotional support of her own mum.

Over 60 million lives had been lost during the war and it was no secret that this resulted in hundreds of thousands of women being widowed. For

Ivy, not knowing the actual whereabouts of Jonny, meant that there was no highly taxed widow's pension from the Government. Bereft and living in a bleak post-war land led Ivy back into a sadness for her daughter. For Iris, there would be no tales of how her father had fought for King and country, earning a vest of medals. There were times when even Ivy's own ability to turn a challenge into and an adventure failed her. Even she couldn't muster up the words to tell Iris that her father's efforts in the war were unknown. There was no way in which she could fabricate tales of his unsung bravery. Equally, she couldn't bring herself to share the stark reality that he chose freedom over family. Who was she to speak the words which would surely sweep Jonny off the pedestal on which Iris had so loyally placed him? Ivy felt a sense of shame as she secretly wondered if there would ever be a young man for her … not even a Prince.

However, Ivy wasn't destined to remain a single mother for too long. Maybe it was some kind of bizarre fate but Ivy was soon introduced to a local widower, who had lost his wife during an air-raid, and was now trying to raise three children by himself. Putting a roof over their heads and ensuring his children were fed and clothed well was no mean feat. Providing them with a new mother was proving to be far more difficult. Of course, there was such an array of "suitable" widows needing financial support and he was quite spoilt for choice. Henry, however, had standards and he often felt weighed down by the responsibility of bringing another woman into the lives of his children. Outweighing this was his own need for company, a good cook and housewife.

Ivy thought it no coincidence that they met at a time when they were in the same boat. Never having lost her penchant for a slick talking man, despite Dot's efforts, she could do far worse than get together with him. Some folk could be forgiven for seeing her as a replacement mum for his children, or that she was a bit of a gold digger. But, even though she couldn't deny the fact that there were financial benefits to their relationship, she had fallen in love. This time, no amount of criticism from Dot would deter her from marrying Henry Dawes. Dot also had a young family to look after and it seemed to Ivy that life with Jonny was too far back in history for people to even try and compare the two men. Whilst both men had similar qualities they were poles apart when it came to taking responsibility. Together, Henry and Ivy would nurture their children with equal amounts of love and attention. In her wildest imaginings, Ivy couldn't see a time when she would face hardship or unhappiness with

Henry. Could she be such a poor judge of character to make the same mistake twice?

Marrying Henry wasn't going to be as simple as she had hoped. Whilst his wife had passed away over a year ago, Ivy had no contact with Jonny and his sister had moved away following D Day celebrations. In essence, he was missing but proving that wasn't easy. How many other women had claimed that their husbands had died during a bombing? Missing in action? That would have been relatively easy but Jonny had not joined the Army as expected and if he had gone to Jersey finding him was going to prove virtually impossible. Applying to the government for help with this wasn't really an option. While Ivy's love for Jonny had dwindled away over the years, something resembling loyalty prevented her from taking any steps which might land him in trouble. Was Jonny lost in Dunkirk, or lost in a chance to shirk?

However, Ivy needed a husband, Iris needed a step-father and Henry's three children needed a step-mother. Whist this was true, Henry's children were actually nearer in age to her than to Iris so "mothering" them was never going to be easy. Again, Ivy deployed her reserves of determination and began to fulfil her role using all the domestic skills her mum had handed down to her. Their home soon became a bustling place to live and, due to the continuation of rationing, her greatest skill was soon proven to be careful budgeting – again.

Having moved to a more suitable house in Southall, life continued to be a bit of a struggle but Ivy was happy all the same. Henry had started his own business as a panel beater and coach-worker and Ivy soon made friends with other women in the area. This helped her to settle Iris and her older siblings (Ivy wouldn't refer to them as Step-children) into schools and jobs. With neighbours such as Mrs Maynard and Mrs Starling – whose' kitchen was just across the rooftops so they could talk from window to window – Western Road quickly became a much needed reprieve from north London for Henry and Ivy. One more than one occasion Ivy noted the similarities between Southall and Mountain Ash. Although there were certainly fewer bridges to Heaven, her new community had adopted the "Dunkirk spirit" and people really did look out for each other. In Wales, Iris had had the luxury of a garden and fields to play in, without a care in the world. In Southall, Ivy became so protective of her and appreciated it when neighbours told her if Iris had been up to mischief. Although in fairness,

Iris didn't get up to mischief. Her idea of being naughty was to pinch the odd chip from Ivy's plate when her head was turned! With that change in environment, Ivy and Henry relaxed into their own form of "married life" (without the marriage). It wasn't long before Ivy found herself expecting another child.

As the loving mother that she was, Ivy enjoyed being a new mum again. The oldest three had since moved on themselves, so they had ample space in the upstairs of their town house for a young family. Iris was now at school, and doing as well as her mum had when she was small. So when daughter number two arrived (and a further four more siblings in years to come) Ivy was in her element. Having retained her curvaceous figure, Ivy was proud to have a lap big enough to sit the "kiddies" on without them having to wait their turn. On more than one occasion Ivy contemplated reinforcing her apron pockets so that she could carry more children around with her. Whatever became of Old Mother Hubbard's pinnie? Cooing or crying made no difference to Ivy, she loved every baby she ever held. In fact it was fair to say that she had such an abundance of love for everyone – and she wasn't afraid to show it. Rather like the penny cascade arcade game she liked, Ivy never ceased to feed her "half-pennies" into the hearts and minds of her babies and didn't ask for any returns. The reciprocated love further fuelled an eternal outpouring from her very being.

Naturally, Ivy soon made it her pleasure to introduce her children to the fun and exercise of swimming. As luck would have it, there was an outdoor swimming pool in the Rec, which was only a ten minute walk away. Armed with a towel and tuppence, she would take the children through the iron turn-stile and head for the pool-side changing cubicles. Somehow it reminded her of the happy times she had spent swimming with Dot at Kensington Road, when life had seemed so simple. Ivy knew she was looking back with rose tinted spectacles but she preferred to think of it as some happier times. To only recall all of the pain and suffering which surrounded her family years before would be a disservice to the freedom and future she had come to appreciate.

With her children in tow, she was soon back in the reality of life as she spent hours splashing in the water and teaching her little ones to swim. It came as no surprise that they were natural water babies and were always reluctant to get out of the pool. However, with frizzle-twisted fingers, they were soon distracted by the promise of a cup of Bovril or extremely thin powdered tomato soup from the kiosk at the top of some stone steps. It never ceased to raise a smile each time Ivy watched her brood go up to the kiosk themselves. The eldest would hold the money at the front and, waiting patiently in line, the younger ones stood on the steps in chronological order. Cups of steaming soup were passed down, along the line before they all made an about turn and filed back to their towels. Her own little synchronised swimming team. Days out at the pool were fun but also served as an opportunity to prepare the children for the choice of pools when they went on holidays to Butlin's. It was there that Ivy could show off her diving skills – joking that she could empty the entire pool (of swimmers and water) as she hit the water.

Whilst ferrying the whole family all the way to Bognor Regis was like a military operation itself, nothing could prevent Ivy from making sure the children had a summer holiday by the sea. There were day trips to the coast at other times but the summer school break, and factory shut down, saw families starting the annual mass migration to the sea. Fleetingly fling south for warmer climes. Clad in brown sandals with hair held fast by Kirby grips, carrying suitcases of an assortment of swimming costumes and sun dresses, the children's incessant chatter seemed to drown out the rhythmic clicked-clack of the railway track. They arrived at the holiday camp excited, if a little pale. They left exhausted, as brown as berries.

Her ever-growing family kept her more than busy as the house became full to the brim again. They had three bedrooms, their own indoor bathroom and a kitchen which served as the hub of the home. Not only did Ivy still cook the most amazing stews and bread puddings on a Saturday, but the room housed the kitchen table, fridge, settee, coal fire and, in years to come, a small portable TV on a shelf in the corner. It wasn't Ivy but her children who questioned Henry as to why they continued to live in such a small space, with two very long staircases to the street and back yard. Moving downstairs to the ground floor flat – which Henry also owned – would have given Ivy more freedom and saved her from battling with the stairs on her tired, withered leg. Over the years it became a bit of a standing joke that Henry had had money enough to move out of North London but continued to go back there every Saturday – saving enough money to buy oranges from Portobello Road market. His own mother being deceased, the children all conceded that he was pulled back by over stretched knicker elastic instead of apron strings.

As he carefully crimped his hair before going, a teenage Iris wondered if that was why his hair stayed so red – he had been eating more oranges than carrots during the war! Not that she would have said this to him. Henry sometimes lacked the same sense of humour as his family. It was just as well that she could share little jokes with her mum, sometimes at her own expense, as this kept the dimples in their cheeks and the sparkle in their eyes.

Despite Ivy's attempts to trace Jonny's whereabouts, it was in vain and Iris and Henry hadn't grown any closer over the years. She couldn't deny the fact that Henry treated her differently to the other children, no matter how hard Ivy tried to rectify it. Ivy just prayed, more than anything, that Iris would meet a man who would treasure her almost as much as she did herself. A Prince would be fantastic but a pauper who loved Iris unconditionally would be even better. Just so long as he didn't whisk her too far away from Southall.

However, Ivy was especially pleased by the way Iris had formed such close friendships with another large family in the area. Meeting Rosie at secondary school had been such a breath of fresh air for Iris. She now had someone her own age outside of the family and Rosie had as more cousins and relatives than Iris could remember, so they had no problem socialising and meeting new people together. Seeing her daughter skipping off arm-in-arm with Rosie, more than warmed her heart. It reminded her of her own teenage years, spent swimming and flirting with fate. Dot may have been in tow back then but they were happy memories, of carefree times. Although, fleeting thoughts of Jonny still crept in, and quickly crept out again. All Ivy could do was to hope and pray that Iris met her soulmate the first time around. She wasn't to be disappointed.

Much to Ivy's pleasure, Iris seemed to be mentioning one of Rosie's many cousins rather a lot and she felt she already knew Richard when Iris brought him home for tea just before her fifteenth birthday. Somehow, Ivy really trusted her own instincts and decided he was a lovely young man – so obviously good enough for her eldest child. Fate gave way to faith and she prayed for a long and happy future for them together.

Four Leaf Clover

Four Leaf Clover

Four Leaf Clover

6   IRIS – THE MOTHER

An ecstatic Iris and Richard Lord proudly announced the arrival of their son, Kenny, a couple of days after their first Christmas as husband and wife. Having had to remove her wedding and engagement rings due to swollen fingers, Richard had slipped a plastic ring from inside her Christmas cracker onto her finger. It was to bring a smile to her face every time she remembered how the midwife had carefully put it into the hospital safety deposit box, as if it were the Koh-I-Noor diamond!

Motherhood was to bring Iris so many more precious memories. As Kenny met the world, dressed in a pale green matinee coat, he instantly became the apple of his parent's eye. He had been blessed with sparkling grey eyes and a hairline which mirrored Iris' widow's peak. Whilst he hadn't arrived with Richard's mop of curls they somehow came to see this as a blessing. Iris had experience at braiding the long hair of her sisters but found the prospect of managing tightly curled hair on her son a little daunting. How she would gain control over bouncy tresses without ribbons and rubber bands was beyond her. What-ever Samsonesque mop of hair he might have lacked, he certainly made up for with sizable lungs – again eluding the constraints of ribbons and rubber dummies. In fact, little could pacify a screaming Kenny. Even the family tradition of dipping his dummy in whiskey failed, briefly, to calm him. Iris refused to accept that he was a demanding baby, ruling the roost from the off. No, to the besotted mum he was a precious, vulnerable babe needing nothing more than the softness and strength she freely gave him.

It seemed to Richard, that his beautiful wife had been born to be a mother. There was no awkward fumbling with terry towelling nappies or complaining when Kenny awoke in the night – several times. Living with

Richard's family had limitations as they attempted to keep the baby crying to a minimum. However, Iris found time to cuddle and coo over their son as well as being a perfect wife. Whilst it wasn't deemed to be the job of a dad to tend to the baby in the night, Richard had all good intentions of doing so but Iris was undoubtedly devoted to her son and husband, as she would always be. Both of them believed that they couldn't love anybody as more as they loved each other but they were ill-prepared for the overwhelming love they instantly felt for Kenny.

It was as a mother that Iris really came into her own. It was true that she still welcomed the support and guidance from Ivy, but there wasn't much which phased her. Despite being a "vocal" baby, Kenny grew and developed as he should and was often compared to her youngest sibling, who had been born in the summer of the same year. Iris found it strange being pregnant at the same time as Ivy and accepted that this was in fact the time when she herself evolved into a woman and mother in almost at once. The wonderful years they had shared in Wales, all those years ago, had seen the beginnings of magical roots and tendrils binding mother and child. Now she felt those tendrils developing into boughs which will never break under the weight of any rock-a-bye baby.

Whilst she was focusing on her devotion to her "boys", Iris (or Richard) hadn't pre-empted the amount of involvement Maud and Edward were to have with raising the baby. They couldn't deny that Maude was more than experienced at rearing a child and, at times, it was a huge help. Kenny wore booties and bonnets knitted by Maud, gowns sewn and embroidered by Maud and was photographed more often than royalty by Edward. To all intents and purposes their help was a boon. However, nothing could detract from Iris' and Richard's dreams of living in their own home and having the other two babies they had planned. With Richard having to do his National Service the plans were understandably and temporarily put on hold. They would continue to enjoy Kenny as he reached all of his milestones earlier rather than later than the average baby. Of course, Iris knew that most parents think their baby is more beautiful and clever than any other child who ever walked the planet. Feeling the motherly pride was, surely a rite of passage, but Kenny really was a bright baby.

Iris was soon to establish her own parenting style of providing for all of Kenny's needs, whilst utilising the invaluable skills she had attained as an older sister. Of all of the family values she had, honesty and integrity were of the utmost importance to her. Ivy had taught her that being true to her own feelings and beliefs was paramount with a child – or in fact in any relationship. She practiced this religiously in her life as a wife and mother and made a resolution to impart this onto her children (convinced she was to bare three children of her own).

There were occasions when she didn't relish the involvement of any of Kenny's grandparents but her placid nature kept her from rebuffing it or seeming ungrateful. One such occasion was when Iris decided to placate a teething Kenny by rubbing a small amount of whiskey on his gums. Maud quickly pointed out that this was an old-fashioned practice which would have long lasting repercussions but Iris stood her ground as she had no evidence of it ever harming her siblings. Secretly, Iris wondered if, with such a large family of men, there hadn't been enough whiskey to go around to "waste" on a baby. She knew this hadn't actually been the case as Richard's own grandfather was teetotal and, despite being a large family, each boy had been nurtured to an almost religious standard.

Despite being warmly welcome in various family houses, Iris and Richard longed for their own home. The plan had been to wait until Richard's wages as a draughtsman could pay for such a house. Saving hard came as a second nature for iris but not quite so for Richard. Having grown up with virtually everything he wanted, he wasn't as accustomed to being frugal as his new wife – or his own parents for that matter. Everyone in the family wanted to indulge Kenny, the way Maud had Richard, but the tides needed to turn if this were to be put into practice.

However, with Kenny fast approaching his third birthday, they were blessed with the arrival of Terry Albert Lord. Needless to say, he was another welcome addition to the family and, despite Iris' promise not to spoil him, he soon became the subject of much love, affection and obligatory photographs taken by Edward.

Terrys' arrival wasn't without problems, however. He had been born with congenital dislocation of the hips and spent most of his early months either in hospital or encased in plaster of Paris to correct his bones. He became no stranger to the barrage of lumbar punctures, blood tests and other invasive procedures which caused him and his parents' great distress. At some stage, although Iris wasn't exactly sure when, Terry became something of the "blue-eyed boy" of the family but this wasn't to have any lasting ramifications. He was a cheeky, funny, accident prone little boy who bought untold joy to Iris and Richard. Inheriting Iris' bright blue eyes, he soon won the hearts of all who knew him and never ceased to entertain people with his antics and adorable ways. To his favourite aunt, he became known as a little Charlie Drake – a comedic actor who never failed to make people laugh with his stunts and funny walks. Even the face he pulled every time Edward photographed him, made Iris and Richard laugh. With one eye screwed into a wink above a crooked grin, it took his parents many, many months to realise that he was, in fact, trying to copy his grandfather's expression. Closing one eye as he expertly focussed his lens.

Knowing no bounds, Terry attacked every single task with an energy and enthusiasm beyond compare. Inevitably, this resulted in as many achievements as accidents – some of which Iris and Richard would prefer not to remember. Some of which would be recounted, with an ever-growing audience, with more than a hint of admiration and pride. Even describing the events which surrounded his several hospital trips Iris's tales were centred on the bravery Terry showed. Surely, a virtue she passed on to him. Loving him in the way she loved Kenny came easy to Iris, even though she had worried that she might not have enough love to give two sons and save some for the daughter they were determined to have. Iris needn't have fretted.

On occasion, Iris would think about her journey to motherhood and the traits she had adopted from Ivy, together with the skills and influences from Maud. It seemed inevitable that she would share some of their family values. It also seemed natural that she would mirror some of their approaches to motherhood, almost to the letter. For example, determined not to have her sons dressed in second-hand clothes led Iris to devote a lot of her spare time to knitting their romper suits and mittens. Whilst this was common practice, it gave her a sense of pride to see them looking cosy and snug in something she had lovingly made for them. The fact that Terry wore some of Kenny's baby clothes surely didn't count as "cast offs"? More like "heirlooms".

However, it was very much her own values which shaped the way she was to impart discipline and rewards, whilst simply doting on her children. Iris certainly had her style when it came to showing tenderness and affection to them which was borne of her own gentleness and loving nature. This wasn't as a result of being a caring older sister, or a helpful daughter, or even a beloved grand-daughter. It was Iris' own unique beauty and natural ability to give unconditional love to her husband and children. Nobody could deny that Ivy had possessed similar qualities but it was Iris who honed them to perfection. Such was her resolve to protect her family and teach them, in turn, to develop these attributes for themselves.

Although Iris and Richard were more than happy, they still had the niggling desire to have their own home. One with a bedroom for their sons, a real bathroom and they even dared to dream of having a little garden to play football in. Not that the boys were particularly good at football, being under five-years-old, but still they dreamed. Saving for a deposit on a house was really stretching their combined budgeting skills. This was something they were determined to do – although Iris was a lot more frugal when it came to unnecessary treats for her sons. It was more than fortuitous that Maud and Edward were in a position to buy them new bicycles and some of the latest toys. Edward and Richard had the philosophy – much like the women in their lives – that their children would have the best they could afford to buy (or at least a carefully hand-crafted replica).

Debt was a word that didn't feature in Iris' vocabulary. She had seen her mum negotiating terms with the "tally man" on occasion which caused Iris some resentment towards her step-father. Whilst Henry wasn't exactly rich, it was widely known that he had enough to support his expanding family and yet he seemed to accept that Ivy felt the need to borrow money on a regular basis. Iris knew this was exactly where she had acquired her aversion to spending beyond her means.

However, she did quite enjoy the weekly ritual of trying to predict the results by "investing in" the football pools, as did Richard. They decided it wasn't really gambling because everyone did it and they waited with baited breath to hear the results on the radio every Saturday teatime. The familiar voice, which rose and fell like their hopes with every score. The reverent silence broken only by the tapping and scraping of poised pens, recording the "Leeds 1 (pause) Chelsea 2" which deflated everyone. Of course nobody ever won more than a shilling or two but it was the excitement and anticipation which gave them all pleasure. Little did they know that someone in the family was going to buck the trend and net themselves an enviable win – Iris and Richard!

Maud would say "you could knock me down with a feather"! Edward would say "spend it wisely" and virtually all of their other friends and relations would say "you lucky beggars. Where's my share?" and Iris and Richard could only just manage to say "a house, a house!"

Beyond their wildest dreams, Richard had won a very impressive £1,300! More than his annual salary, more than any amount of dedicated saving would ever have amounted to. Or, if it had, they would probably be too old to raise their children and would end up skipping a generation in order to help with their grand-children. It was true that Richard was earning a reasonable wage by then but money had been tight recently. Maud and Edward only accepted a small contribution to the running of the household. Neither Richard or Iris were drinkers, she smoked occasionally, Richard shared the pleasures of photography with is dad. Their outgoings were reasonably low but raising the boys was still an expense – one that they relished.

Whilst the young family were happy, cocooned within the love and support from everyone, they yearned for a house of their own.

So, with a good work ethic, extremely respectable deposit and a regular income their dreams were soon to come into fruition. Richard had duly secured a mortgage for their own house and they wasted no time in searching for the house in the country they had dreamed of for so long. Wearing hats of hope and coats of courage, they set off along their long and happy journey together.

Maybe Hillingdon wasn't exactly in the countryside but it was at least two bus rides away from where they had both grown up, and it had three bedrooms and the much longed for garden – all 100 feet of it! Wide wooden gates led into the driveway and a smaller gate stood to the left, like a gate-in-waiting. A tidy garden lay to the front, a welcome mat larger than the entire bedroom they had shared in Dudley Road.

The tiny hallway ushered visitors into the living room, warmed by autumn sunlight. Smells of lino and coal fire mingled in the air between this room and the kitchen. It was a galley kitchen, narrow and long, bathed in natural light from a small window at the end. A window which lifted the mouth-watering aromas of wholesome meals which Iris was to serve to her family. The family could eat in their very own dining room. Two reception rooms. Or as Iris liked to say "a room for greeting and a room for eating"!

It seemed to Iris that this labyrinth flowed on and on, to a place far beyond her wildest dreams. Up the stairs, the walls curved onto a landing, acting as a buffer zone around the three bedrooms. Waiting to cradling her family in eiderdowns and candlewick bed spreads. Then there was the bathroom. Their own bathroom. An indoor bathroom with tiles, a sink and a basin as well as a window with special bobbly glass. Even the neighbours were kept from sharing this room, let alone many much-loved relatives.

Together, Richard and Iris explored the corners and crevices of their new home. Marvelling at the "grown-upness" of having such an amazing house, they each started to visualise how they would furnish it. From the red polished doorstep at the front to the stone back doorstep and the French doors of the dining room, Iris was to build a nest fit for the most precious Lords. Richard drank in the smells of oil and wood of the garage – a real garage! It was here he was to store his car and tins of paint left over from carefully decorating their home. However, just as excited as Richard, Edward was overwhelmed at the sight of a work-shed at the end of the garden. Iris just about managed to steal a peep at her husband and father-in-law as they set about exploring it, like the men she hoped her sons would grow up to be.

This house was where they would raise their own special family. A home which would keep them safe, warm and happy. Richard would paint the front door and Iris would hang brilliant white net curtains at the windows. Each window sporting the same lacy pattern, in perfect folds, caressed into place with love.

However blissful this was, what mattered the most was the support they had from their respective parents. And the opportunity to introduce Kenny and Terry to their very own room. The third bedroom, it was small but the perfect size for the little girl Iris just knew she would have.

It was then that Iris made a pact with herself to give her children the childhood she had so wanted for them. They would have space for toys, bicycles and maybe even a go-cart which they would build with Richard's help. Edward could take their photographs to his heart's content as the boys played in make-shift tents. Iris would arrange birthday parties for them and, the most precious memory she would help to make would be Christmas in their very own home.

With Christmas decorations, from Woolworths, hanging from corner to corner, and a sweet smelling pine tree in the corner, Iris took unrivalled care in dressing the front room for the festive season. Tissue paper lanterns swooped down into the room, held up by paperchains secured with children's spit. Sitting in a circle and looping the paper strips almost became a race to see who could produce the longest chain, with the most colours. More than once, Kenny and Terry would fight over the chain links. Terry invariably won the battle as he was more adept at squirrelling supplies under his chubby knees, only to produce them when Kenny had exhausted his "share". These were such times which made Iris swell with pride. Not necessarily at her own achievement of having two wonderful boys. It was outweighed by the knowledge that they each had a sibling to grow and learn with, something which Richard valued immensely.

Moving into their first home went well, with most of their furniture being given to them. The main exception was the burgundy and grey boucle three piece suite. They belonged together, five safe seats, waiting for five members of the same precious family. Iris could wait for her family to reach five.

Iris started her Christmases as she meant to go on. There would be no second-hand clothes under their tree and no "donated" baubles in her house. Gifts purchased from Southall Broadway were wrapped in sheets of paper from good old Woollies. Each child having equal numbers of gifts to open on Christmas morning. So, it came as no surprise to Richard that Iris enlisted his help with placing their very own angel on top of the tree, after she had draped a delicate dark red, paper garland around the branches – with as much precision he himself used as a draughtsman. Only then would Iris allow him to relax and put his feet up before Father Christmas had to start his rounds.

This Christmas was memorable for another reason. It was 1962 and the following spring was to bring them baby number three. There was no scientific way of predicting the sex of the baby but plenty of "old wives' tales" had started many a discussion between Iris, her mother and virtually every woman in the neighbourhood! In fact, before Iris had even become pregnant again, her Grandmother had mentioned that she would love to have seen Iris' family complete with a daughter. Iris had been close to her Grandmother and her words never left her. She was naturally devastated when her grandmother passed away on 21st April 1962. With those words ringing in her ears, exactly twelve months later, Iris found great comfort in "knowing" that she was carrying a baby girl.

The New Year of 1963 came in the guise of unprecedented snow storms which prevented Iris and Richard from making their weekly trips to Southall. They missed seeing their families, chatting as the women knitted yet more baby booties and the men talked earnestly about football (although Richard still preferred cricket). It was time to go when their bellies were full of stew and crossword puzzles were complete. As comforting and fulfilling as these Saturdays were, Iris still got excited as they drove nearer and nearer to their home in Weald Road.

Choosing not to believe the old wives' tales, but the final wishes of her Grandmother, Iris knew that the arrival of their daughter was meant to be. The harsh winter chills gave way to delicate spring sunshine, bringing warmth to the cherry blossom and daffodils in their garden. A ray of sunshine.

Jill arrived on a Sunday afternoon, in their bedroom at 10 Weald Road, whilst Richard waited on tender hooks downstairs. His anxious pacing making little or no sound, left Richard ready to bound up the stairs at the sweet screams of his daughter. Together, Iris and Richard marvelled at her rosy cheeks and wispy dark hair they knew, in their hearts, that their baby (born on the Sabbath day) would certainly be "good and blithe and bonny and gay".

Iris was never really sure how she came to be named Jill. Richard had been the one to register her birth, and she wondered if it was either after his favourite nursery rhyme or because they had shared such a cold winter with Jack Frost! Either way, they fell in love with her the moment she was born and that day in April 1963 started with unrivalled pride and affection. True to form, as soon as the shops at Crescent Parade opened on Monday, Richard rushed there and bought Jill's first teddy bear. It was a little brown, Wendy Boston bear which Jill would treasure well into her adult life. There was no doubt that Iris had enough love to go round her three little ones, she needn't have worried, because they were all such amazing individuals who brought varied and priceless contributions to her world.

Like her brothers before her, Jill brought moments of delight and humour as well as some very testing antics. The least of all was when

Richard discovered a trail of perfect, tiny footprints on the garden path. Curiosity curdled with trepidation as he followed the trail. Would he find Hansel, Gretel or an errant seagull? Unless seagulls wore Jumping Jacks that wasn't very likely. As he peered into the garage, letting his eyes adjust to the darkness, he spotted the culprit. He saw a chubby, smiling toddler who was totally oblivious of the spreading puddle of paint which surrounded her. Richard couldn't be cross with her, just cross with himself that he didn't have his camera to hand.

Jill also appeared to lack a certain level of intelligence when she spilled the entire contents of her bottle on the driveway and paddled in the milk. She was soon forgiven for both antics – she was only two at the time.

Apart from preparing for Christmas, some of Iris' favourite times were the family outings they took together. Whether it was a trip to Richmond Park to see the deer or further afield to Banbury (where Richard and Iris had spent days taking a break from his National Service duties) they always had fun. With the boys dressed in identical outfits (new, of course) and Jill sporting her latest frock, they all climbed into their estate car as Richard proudly drove them along country lanes and A roads. To the all too common cries of "are we there yet", Iris would reply with an eye-spy clue which distracted them however briefly.

It was to be some years before Jill sat in a small stripy child car seat. Until then, she had travelled either on Iris' lap or in her carry cot – in the boot! When Iris saw the little seats in the shops she just had to have one for Jill. Wide hooks looped over the back of the rear seats to secure it before she was allowed to climb into it. Thin white webbing straps were fastened around her middle and she was ready for the off. Not only did it make for a safer journey, but Iris could turn to see her little girl beaming at the big wide world of passing scenery. The children might have squabbled about who was going to sit in the middle (with limited leg room) but the sight of them all in a row never ceased to bring a smile to her face.

Although the car, and finances, didn't quite meet the demands for the trips to France which they had dreamed of, the proud parents were determined to take the children on an annual holiday. This wasn't to keep up with the neighbours, it was more about giving their children experiences which would enrich their lives. Building memories had become dearly valued by Richard as well. Although the recording of such experiences were mostly afforded to his own emerging photography skills. The technology which brought cine cameras into his hands had mixed blessings as far as Iris was concerned.

Gone were the times when she could take a moment or two to straighten her skirt or smooth down a wayward wisp of hair from Jill's face. The cine camera pried and peered into her face, uninvited and sometimes unwanted, snatching away her privacy and replacing it with reels of colourless silent movies. Any animosity quickly melted away with the raucous laughter ringing in peels around the house when they were played back. The family would gather in excitement as Richard fed the film through the projector, onto the big screen (or wall). With the children sitting cross legged on the floor, scenes of sand dunes and, swimmers flickered around them as they recognised themselves. Even Iris had to laugh herself as each time she realised that Richard was filming her she shooed him away with a comical "cross face".

The film shows were also a way of extending the holiday. Watching themselves, the children would point out how big and better their sandcastles became each year. They never seemed to notice that the films were in black and white. Iris, on the other hand, remembered each and every outfit her "babies" had been dressed in. For the boys it was yellow swimming trunks (matching) and for Jill it was a pink and white gingham dress, with pink pleats. Her outfit may not have been colour coordinated with her brothers, but Iris always saw to it that Jill's knickers matched her dress.

Be it in Dimchurch or Camber Sands the holidays were always filled with fun and laughter. One of their favourite journeys was the long, but interesting, drive to the West coast. With the Kenny and Terry settled on the back seats and Jill safely ensconced in her carry-cot (and, later in her stylish seat) they set off in the early hours of the morning. Taking the A303 was the only route so it made sense that Richard would drive as far as Stonehenge and they would stop for breakfast as the sun came up. Iris wasn't quite sure when she introduced the steadfast ritual of making a picnic of tuna and tomato sandwiches but it was to be a legacy which was welcomed by all of her descendants. With a sprinkle of salt and a drizzle of vinegar they were essential for *any* journey. Soggy bread an 'all.

One thing Iris was certain of was the way Kenny and Terry liked to play tricks on Jill. She remembered one such occasion when they were staying in a caravan in Kent. Every evening there would be a visit from the "bin men" who drove a tractor towing a huge rubbish cart. Unknown to their parents, the boys had told Jill that the tractor was actually collecting children and this caused her immeasurable distress. As the cart came nearer, the spluttering of the engine and the rumble of the huge tyres as they thundered towards her – or their caravan – barely drowned out her screams. Sheer fear and desperation rooted her to the spot. The relief when they drove right passed her was almost palpable. It was several days before Iris and Richard could calm her enough to get to the bottom of the incident. Needless to say, the brothers were duly chastised but the damage had been done.

It was no surprise that Iris was a protective mum, as would be expected, and most people saw her as the demure, passive woman that she was. However, for those who dared to criticise or harm her children she showed a feistiness second to none. With startling ferocity, she would leap to their defence, making it perfectly clear that any threat to her brood was not going to be tolerated. Never once did she resort to physical confrontation. Iris didn't need to. Her piercing blue eyes would deliver "the look", which was usually reserved for errant children.

This would be accompanied by a rather eloquent tirade of superlatives, resulting in her opponent feeling embarrassed and defeated. Not one profanity would leave her lips, but woe betide anyone who threatened her babies.

As the three of them grew older, it wasn't unheard of for Iris to ask the boys to look after Jill for a while – or at least take her to the park with them. Weald Road was home to a few children of similar ages and the older ones didn't complain much. True to form, this provided them with an opportunity to subject Jill to another one of their pranks. It was the very hot summer of 1976. Bush fires were sweeping across the arid areas of the country. Children became as parched as the grass in the gardens but, as was the norm, were encouraged to go out and play, to get some fresh air in their lungs. To get some colour in the cheeks. On one such day, all three little Lords had ventured into the field where an orchard was being replaced with a new housing estate. In previous occasions they had spent hours scrumping in the orchard. It was a real achievement to grab handful of apples and make it back to the safety of the fence before the geese caught them. A haven of grappling friends, helping each other to scramble away from the gaggle of guard geese.

On one such occasion, they had met up with friends and neighbours and found themselves at a loss for what to do for entertainment. Voting to go to Court Drive Park, some twenty minutes' walk away, the boys were faced with how to avoid taking Jill with them whilst letting Iris think she was safe with them. A tag-along girl would be a real pain, from the moment they set off on Long Lane, until she could be bribed to stop moaning with an ice-pop. However, Jill leaped at the suggestion of playing hide and seek. She was a bit reluctant to find a hiding place as they weren't supposed to be on the building site in the first place. Hearing of Jill's dilemma, Kenny – the ever thoughtful brother – told her to climb onto the porta-cabin roof, using the open door struts as a ladder. He assured her that nobody would think to look there for her. Obviously, he was right. Jill lay there for what seemed like hours, in the blistering heat, alone and a bit scared, whilst the group of boys headed to the park in the shade. When they eventually came back for her they deliberately omitted to tell her about how they had washed their feet in the cold water of the park ditch. If anyone needed an orange Mivvi lolly it was Jill, not her brothers as they lay under the cool branches of spreading oak trees.

And so it went on. Brothers playing tricks on sisters, whilst mothers were unaware. A childhood of fun and frolics which morphed back and forth between taunts and treats. Of course, the other thing Iris would pride herself on, as a mother, was the fact that her daughter would never have to wear her brother's hand-me-downs!

Four Leaf Clover

7   PART TWO

Four Leaf Clover

8   JILL - THE GRANDDAUGHTER

Just how much her grandparents doted on her wasn't written across the skies, but they did, all the same. She just knew she was the apple of their eye – although she often looked intently for, but missed, the said apple. From a very young age she was aware of that her two grandmothers were quite different. Time that she spent with Ivy was invariably shared with aunties, uncles, cousins or cats. This wasn't a problem. Her time spent with Maud was quiet and calm, just the two of them. This wasn't a problem. It was just the way it was.

In truth, there was no comparison to the way Jill loved each of her grandmothers. Each nurturing her love of all things shiny and beautiful, and each nurturing her love of food!

Saturdays were a special day for Jill and her family. This was when they would travel all the way to Southall, usually by bus, arriving at Maud's for a much needed drink of cherryade. Sometimes she was even lucky enough to be there when the Corona man came and Jill would carry out the empty bottles with great care and importance – returning with the penny refund tightly held in her grasp. Only to hand it over to Maud and into the kitty for next week.

Maud usually bought a few different flavours of fizzy drinks from the Corona man in his cart. Jill knew that there wasn't always enough money for the favourite flavours of her and her two brothers in the same week. Although she struggled to be patient when it was dandelion and burdock week, she was duly reminded that her brothers has also been patient waiting for cherryade week to pass. Cream soda week often sneaked in too, Jill not being entirely sure who could like the sweetness of the bubbles. Somehow, she thought, the bubbles were bigger in cream soda and must surely be related to the bubbles in the sea. The way they softly tickled her toes before disappearing, shyly, into the sand. The way they popped against the side of the glass before disappearing, sneakily into the cold liquid.

There was a similar system with the crisps, which Maud kept in a square tin. It had served as a biscuit tin in a previous life. Nestled firmly inside were four packets of Smiths crisps, four different flavours. Again, they were purposefully chosen to meet the tastes of Jill and her brothers. Cheese and onion for her, Bovril for Terry and salt and vinegar for Kenny. Every week the fourth packet stayed in the tin, the metal lid closed firmly to keep it safe from whatever dangers might be lurking in the pantry. Jill knew that whatever it was, IT liked Smiths crisps too because the following week there would be a different fourth flavour. It just might be possible, she thought, that there was a monster so fierce and hungry that it was strong enough to break into the tin, gobble up the crisps – wrapper and all – swapping it for a new packet each week. If this was the case, Jill wondered, why her Grandmother wasn't afraid to go into the spidery tomb. Miss Manners must live there. Jill never asked for the fourth packet.

The crisp tradition, or ritual, preceded their visit to Ivy's for lunch. Less than a mile away, the walk was, by and large, uneventful. There were several roads to cross, including the street where her dad's auntie lived. Occasionally they would visit her, with Maud, in her little terraced house. That house also seemed to be occupied by a mysterious tenant, which lurked behind the dark curtains at the bottom of the stairs. The problem with this house was that Jill had to pass the curtain in order to get from one room to another, without getting attacked. Most of the time she managed to spend the whole visit in the front room, playing with a china salt and pepper set. She had no doubt that there were more interesting things in the back but, for her own safety, she would spend hours watching the little black and white pots toddle down the slope in front of the fireplace. It never occurred to her that this was a strange place to keep condiments, let alone ones which walked. The gentle tapping sound they made on their fateful journey down was to be as comforting as ever when she recalled it some fifty years later.

Further along was Western Road, extremely busy in comparison to the quiet streets and avenues of Hillingdon. Clutching her mother's hand tightly, Jill struggled to refrain from running, top speed, across the road instead of briskly walking with Iris. Huge lorries carrying bricks enough to build a whole town, thundered around the bend, wafting a smelly cloud of diesel and grease into their faces. A sickly stink of engine oil, over powering the comforting aroma of the paraffin and plywood, which usually floated out from the adjacent hardware shop. Jill would come to resent the way the cloying stench of diesel robbed her of this sensory link to Edward. Heavy fumes weighing down the floating dust of fresh wood, suffocating smells and memories. The wheels were even bigger than the young Jill and filled her with dread as she teetered on the kerb every Saturday. Bigger, even, than the tyres of the child-catching rubbish cart.

Welcoming her on the other side of the road was the sanctity of Ivy's. The place where the door was always open, literally. With a call of "it's only me", Iris would lead her up the steep staircase and into the back room. Red linoleum held in place by metal rods, covered the stairs and tiny landing. Tufts of matting sprung from the edges. Stopping abruptly at the door to the living room, it gave way to a much more cheerful flooring. In fact, Jill found the whole room cheerful. It was a hive of activity and her Nan was the queen bee. Not that her Nan didn't work hard, it was the exact opposite. She would be bustling around the stove, while Iris chopped vegetables at the blue Formica table. Aunts would pass clinking plates across the room, performing the dance of worker bees, never colliding. From somewhere within this circus of organised chaos, Ivy could be heard calling her family to the table. With so many to feed it was no surprise that she went through the entire family tree before she called out the name of the child, grandchild, and daughter in law, who was being summoned to eat. Confusion quickly giving way to infectious laughter. It was some years before Jill really appreciated this, as a mum herself, but she laughed as loud as any.

From the moment she was born, Jill loved her food. She especially loved the food that Ivy cooked and it didn't go un-noticed by her that Iris made dishes as wholesome and delicious at home. As if by magic, a plate of soggy dumplings swimming in thick, dark gravy appeared in front of her. Icebergs of cauliflower nestled among the orange carrots, letting off steam which danced all the way to her nostrils. Genies of temptation.

Unfortunately for Jill, eating at Ivy's had to come to an end. This meant so much more than the thought of "going hungry" until teatime at Maud's. It meant the cascading washing up water was flushed away, along with the gravy which clung loyally to the plates. It meant her senses were about to be assaulted by the cloying stench of perm lotion. Ammonia stung her eyes. Rotten eggs (to Jill) plugged her nose and threatened to eradicate any trace of dinner from her mind. This was where Jill's imagination and memory became a real saving grace. Even the thought of having to cross the roads between trucks which bulldozed through her day, couldn't crush the recollection of such amazing culinary delights. She would just have to bide her time until the bread pudding was ready!

Of course, Ivy didn't spend all day churning out delicious food. Jill looked forward to Saturdays because this was the day her spit was needed. Licking the backs of Green Shield stamps and sticking them into the printed squares of the savings book gave her so much pleasure. Stiff with dried saliva, the books soon grew fat enough to be exchanged for household items. Travelling all the way to Hounslow was an exciting outing for Jill. Not only did she get to see her hard work come to fruition, in the guise of kitchen scales or kettles. To Jill, this was an occasion when she was out with the women of the family. Not at home with the children.

The house in Western Road was always welcoming and homely. Warmth emanated from Ivy's embrace, with only the coal stove in competition. Jill knew which she preferred, from a very early age. The stove crackled and smoked, scary red eyes peering out of the tiny window, waiting to suck little girls into its burning belly. Ivy's lap softened and squished as she climbed up into her arms. The smells of baking in her hair and pinafore. Blue eyes dancing an invitation to come closer for a cuddle. Nobody ever shouted out "mind Nanny's lap – you'll get hurt"!

It wasn't in Ivy's lap, but one Saturday Jill did get hurt. Their regular trips to the swimming pool were always filled with fun if not sun. Soon after their arrival, the pool-side changing cubicles were occupied by Jill's relatives so she invariably had to change by the actual pool-side. This didn't bother her as she was usually ready before everyone else. Not that she could get into the water before the others. Iris and Ivy both made sure she was adorned with water wings, which resembled an inflatable white swan, before going near the pool. At the tender age of five, Jill hadn't mastered swimming unaided like the rest of her family. One day she might inherit the aquatic skills of her mum and Nan, but not until she had experienced the dangers of still water.

The golden rule was that Jill had to stay in the shallow end of the pool, with her water wings on. Most of the time she kept to the rules. However, on this occasion, Jill had slipped out of the swan's embrace and deep into the water. Miraculously she had managed to grab the rail at the side of the water just before she sank beneath the surface. With elbows linked through the metal bars, Jill was making a valiant attempt to get herself back to the safety of the shallow end. She hadn't been prepared for what happened next. As she slid along, her arms were prized away from the side and she found herself being pushed far into the pool by her water-baby uncle. Out of her depth, Jill instantly sank back deep into the water. With arms and legs flailing manically, she started to rise to the surface. Through the water she could just about see the red of the life guard's shirt, framed by the blurry blue skies behind him. Jill was edging closer to help with each kick. Just as quick as she floated upwards, she began spiralling back down into the depths. Again, her frantic moves brought her skywards. Chlorinated water poured into her mouth, stifling her scream for help. With only enough time to either breathe or shout, her survival instinct took over. Kicks became stronger, her arms pulled at the water with panic until she rose again. From out of the sky, strong hands swept her up and swung her onto the warm concrete of the poolside. As he carried her to the safe haven of Iris' arms, the life guard let the water from Jill's lungs fall and mingle with the perspiration on his shirt.
This close brush with death never left Jill's memory and fuelled fear of water for many years to come.

Saturdays extended into weeks when it came to the summer holidays. Jill was too young to understand the significance of waiting until the schools broke up when she started to pester Iris about how long until they went to Butlin's. She could, however, read the tell-tale signs that the time was looming. Iris would be busy buying and folding new clothes for her children. For Jill, it meant new socks and dresses sewn by Iris in fabric carefully chosen from reams of floral cotton. Three pairs of jelly shoes, three sun hats, three pairs of shorts. Three well turned out Lords. Jill felt so important in her new seer sucker swimsuit but never really fathomed out why Richard had badgered Iris to fork out on new trunks for the boys each year.

For the duration of their stay, Jill's attention wavered between playing in the cold water fountain and hurrying into the dining hall three times a day. With the memory and sound of her weak, drowning gasps, ringing in her ears she avoided going into the water whenever possible. However, no matter how loud the fountain water rushed into her ears, nothing could muffle the two-tone bing bong which echoed around the camp – announcing food! Jill even enjoyed the insipid chicken soup which spilled from her spoon, like her very own fountain. Whilst she lapped up every meal served, Jill knew it was far, far removed from the delights which appeared on her plate at home. Far removed from the mouth-watering meals which appeared on the plate at Ivy's. What she couldn't have known, as such a young child, was that she would, one day, make stews and dumplings appear on the plates of her own children.

The relationship Jill had with Maud was different, but just as special, all the same. Whilst Iris took the children back to Maud's for tea, every Saturday, it was a whole different experience. Jill wasn't met by sweet or savoury smells as she stepped into the long hall. It too had a soft feel but it was grey, floral carpet (which didn't meet the edges). There weren't any steep stairs to fly up, but a staircase which was sent winding upwards, leading to three bedrooms. Half way up there was a huge cabinet, built into the alcove, glazed windows protecting carefully folded linen. The resemblance to a haberdasher's cabinet didn't go un-noticed by the young Jill.

Stepping into the back room had some similarities to Ivy's house, such as the fact that the table occupied the majority of the room. The dining chairs didn't match. There was a coal fire. There were windows on one wall. Although Jill didn't exactly play "spot the difference", that just about summed it up.

It wasn't any less homely though. Either side of the fireplace, were two winged armchairs. Jill was to treasure the memories of sitting on Edward's leggy lap as he told her fantastic stories of ugly ducks turning into graceful swans. She was transfixed and hung on his every word, oblivious to the skin on her legs absorbing the red glow of the flickering flames of the coal fire. Edward fed her imagination whilst Maud fed her belly.

That was another thing. The smells which wafted around Maud's kitchen were so different. Often, Jill would have been playing in the garden for some while before she was called to the table for tea. More often still, there weren't any smells coming from the scullery. The table always wore a multi-coloured coat of salad, pickles, freshly cut bread and cold meats. Terry loved corned beef, Kenny loved pickled onions, Jill loved ham. Or she usually did, at home. Whenever Maud laid ham on the plate Jill's nostrils were instantly twitching with desperation to seek out the smell of beetroot, even lettuce. Surely her grandma hadn't deliberately bought sour ham? At least it smelled sour to Jill. Even Maud chose not to eat it, opting for tiny slices of Nimble bread, topped with cottage cheese and cucumber instead. Even Miss Manners would have been suspicious of the bad ham and would have welcomed the times when it was accompanied by a dollop of bubble and squeak. Then her sense of smell was rewarded with the wonderful aroma of left over mashed potato and cabbage being swaddled in a coat of smoking hot beef dripping.

Meal time's aside, Jill loved being with Maud. It was true that she seemed to favour her brothers but Iris had told her that Maud didn't know much about the differences between raising boys and raising girls. One day, when the time was right, Jill planned to tell her Grandma that boys were the ones with willies.

Being Maude's only granddaughter came with so many advantages. Learning to knit from across the room at Ivy's was good but, sitting inches away from Maud as she showed her how to cast on was better. If Jill dropped a stitch or two she could simply ask Maud to help her find it. Making this same mistake at her Nan's house, saw her murmurings for help being carried away by the incessant chatter and laughter which always bounced around the room. In truth, Jill's favourite knitter was her own mum. Iris could create such intricate patterns which turned into beautiful cardigans or blankets before her very eyes. Her fingers seemed to jive to the increasing tempo of her clicking knitting needles. Maud could knit and crochet amazing toys and clothes as well. Like Iris, she was always for making something for someone else – usually Jill and her brothers, or the many unborn babies of both families. If Jill had really taken the time to look, she would have spied a hand-knitted tea cosy, oven glove, toilet roll covers, and draught excluders and so it would continue.

When Jill wasn't inside watching Maud be creative, she loved being in Maud's garden. There was a narrow verge either side of the long path, supporting the tiny picket fence of the flower beds. Welsh poppies stood protectively above shy forget-me-nots, peering through the furry leaves of the antirrhinums. They danced up high whenever there was a gentle breeze, as easily as they bowed down in the presence of a tiny sparrow. Jill loved these flowers above all of the others in Maud's garden. Not only did they appear to be standing on parade for her visits but she could play with them too. Many times she sat with Maud by the little fence, searching for poppies disguised by pixy hats waiting to "pop off" – with some help from her dimpled fingers. Or there were the bunny rabbits which twitched their noses when she gently squeezed them. Forget-me-nots were simply garden jewels.

The wonders of this garden went on. Near the end, on the left, stood Edward's work dusty shed. Although he had passed away when she was seven years old, the familiar smells of sawn wood and epoxy resin never failed to whisk her back to another fond memory. Of the times she spent perched high on a stool, firmly outside the shed as he worked his magic with the wood he always seemed to have. Jill had probably been sitting on the same stool when Edward told her about a little boy, in a foreign country, who went blind following an accident in his own grandfather's workshop. She just knew it wasn't one of his usual tales, told to entertain and amuse her, but she knew it was a story which was meant to keep her safe instead. It must have been true, she decided, because Richard spoke about the same boy when she sat on the very same stool, outside his own dusty workshop, in Weald Road.

It was also to be many years later, that Jill was to learn that the mound of earth opposite the shed was more than a huge flower bed. Standing some inches above her head, Jill rarely clambered up to sit on the top. Letterbox gardens, separated by uniformed hurdles stretched as far as she could see from up there. Cats balancing on fences provided little entertainment as Jill expected them to fall off at any moment. Landing splattered in the alley. Although she was tempted to sit and wait for such a tragedy, even if only to check out whether cats really do land on all-fours. That's where her survey ended – she definitely didn't want to be the one to share curiosity with such an ill-fated creature. So Jill climbed down from the mound of earth and moss which concealed the remnants of the old Anderson shelter, where Maud and baby Richard had found safety – in the olden days.

Also, unlike Ivy, Maud would sometimes babysit Jill and her brothers' over-night. Iris and Richard were young, in love and had a busy social life when money permitted. Coming from two such big families it was no wonder that they either went to or hosted house parties – sometimes letting their children join in too. But on the occasions when this wasn't practical, Maud was more than pleased to have all three grandchildren to stay. Despite her being the only one left living in the house following the loss of her dear father, grandfather and beloved Edward, Maud kept it as homely as ever. She had felt little guilt at her relief when her brothers each found themselves wives and moved out of what had seemed like cramped conditions. Subsequently, she could give the boys a separate bedroom from Jill and indulge her slightly. Jill knew this (because Iris told her) and she was more than pleased to have her own room to sleep in at Maud's, just like she did at home.

A night at Dudley Road bore no other resemblance to a night at home – for many reasons. Before bed-time, Jill would watch her grandma lay a single place at the table, probably for the elusive Miss Manners. They would then climb the stairs, passed the linen cabinet, and Maud would tuck her into a big bed with a kiss on her head. On more than one occasion, Jill would marvel at the length of the single bed. She wondered if she would eventually grow long enough so that her feet could touch the cold metal frame at each end. Her own little bed at home, had been fashioned from oak and necessity because her box room had been too tiny to accommodate even the smallest of beds from the shops. Iris had claimed that second-hand beds were bad for a child's posture anyway.

Having been tucked tightly under the white sheets, Jill was gently reminded that the poet was just under the bed, in case she needed to go in the night. Invariably, she did need to "go" in the night and dutifully pulled the china pot from under the bed.

Hovering over it in a steady squat which Iris would have been proud of, Jill soon filled the pot almost to the brim. The very same brim which caught on her nightdress and promptly tipped the entire contents onto the thick, wool carpet. Maud was far from amused when she stepped in the spreading wet patch in the morning. Jill hoped that she saw it less like wee but more like spilled milk. Maud didn't cry anyway.

It was possible that this wouldn't have happened during a sleep over at Ivy's, purely because she had a proper indoor toilet and bathroom. However it *had* happened at Maud's and, whilst it wasn't to be forgotten, the incident became second only to the night of the beetroot.

As usual, it had been a Saturday and Jill felt the need to disguise the taste of the ham with piles of pickled beetroot. Maud hadn't noticed just how quickly the contents of the jar were disappearing. Nobody could fail to see the speed with which it came shooting out of Jill's mouth in the night. That was the night when Jill learned that beetroot stains pale blue pillow cases for ever, even if they are hand-made by a grandmother.

As Jill grew so did her relationships with her Nan and Grandma. Each woman continued to enrich her life with new skills and experiences, still in differing ways. The jovial atmosphere at Ivy's in contrast to the peaceful space at Maud's. Jill valued both houses and loved both women equally. She was aware of the inevitable differences between the only granddaughter in the family, as opposed to one of so many that Jill didn't know their names (which had nothing to do with the way her Nan recited the entire alphabet until she found the correct name when speaking to one of them!). Whilst Maud could afford to buy her a stunning gold necklace for her thirteenth birthday, it was treasured as much as the Jackie annual which Ivy bought her that Christmas. Ivy let her help with the cryptic crosswords on a Saturday; Maud let her help to polish the brass ornaments on the mantelpiece. Maud let her sit on the vibrating Hoover Spinarinse when she was doing the laundry; Ivy let her turn the handle of the mangle when she was doing the laundry. Finances might have been at opposite poles but love and sticky tape bound them all together in the middle.

These childhood years spun along without Jill having any notion of time, or of how short life apparently was. It was a time when seasons and celebrations took turn in marking eras and years. Whether it be the bitter winter which dusted her face with and icing of snow; or the blistering summer sun which seemed to keep the hot air suspended just above the grass in a haze of tranquillity; Jill looked forward to all four seasons bringing such differing excitements.

Of course, there were the snow drifts of February. They seemed to appear like clouds from the sky, frozen by and for Jack Frost. Settling and hardening in his very own landscape so that he could get up to all the mischief talked about over breakfast bowls of gloopy porridge. For some reason, this seemed to irritate Maud more than Ivy. Probably because she had to venture out into the slippery world, risking an embarrassing and painful fall. Ivy was more house-bound than Maud due to her weakening heart and unsteady gait. Each of them wrapped up in knitted bed jackets and woolly socks at night. In a bizarre unison they piled layer upon layer of clothes on themselves and their respective off-spring, and Jill. The only difference between them was that Maud resembled a Russian doll, retaining her waistline. Ivy seemed to take on the persona of a huggable snowman, in a warm woollen coat with brightly coloured buttons – the pieces of coal glowing in the grate.

Having ensured that her grandchildren had each consumed a bowl of hot cereal, Maud would look on as Jill and her brothers built an impressive snowman which spanned the garden path, otherwise redundant in the icy conditions. No matter how hard she looked, Jill couldn't see the Readybrek halo of orange heat which was supposed to protect her from the bitter winds. Hand knitted mittens offered no protection for the wet either, or cold snow, as they rolled and moulded until the trio were satisfied with their creation.

Jill might have contributed more to the moulding part, she wasn't a fan of strenuously rolling lumps of snow into huge balls which were too heavy to lift. Maybe, one day, she would build her own little snow baby?

Ivy's long yard may have been spacious enough for a whole family of snow people but Jill's construction skills had usually been exhausted in Maud's garden before she visited Ivy. Even if she had ventured down the steep back stairs, Ivy – or anyone – couldn't have watched her play as they would have had to perch carefully on the freezing coal bunker. Alternately, upstairs by the draughty bathroom window which overlooked the yard, or balance on the toilet to look out of the tiny window. Jill couldn't remember this happening.

And so, winter days spent with Ivy consisted of being cocooned in a haven of sensory delights. The coal fire tapping at her ears as it spat and crackled. Her fingers gently caressing the smoothness of the wooden arms of the chairs which were warmed by the nearby flames. A feast of home-cooked foods, feeding her through her eyes before Jill even tasted a morsel. If a stew wasn't simmering in the corner, a bread pudding was baking in the oven – emerging like a farrowed field which would quickly be dressed in its own winter coat of crunching sugar.

Spring came along with a different range of pleasures for Jill. The run up to her birthday in April was sprinkled with the distraction of Mother's Day gifts and Easter eggs. Many celebrations in her life were influenced by various events in the Christian calendar and Easter was to be her favourite throughout her years.

Jill was completely aware that Maud and Ivy weren't her mother's but she gave them gifts all the same. Without fail, February would see her washing two small yoghurt pots which she would lovingly paint and wait for years for them to dry. They were always blue. Under the watchful eye of Iris, she would fill them to the brim with dark, soft earth and poke a couple of papery onions as deep down as her chubby fingers would allow. Watered and watched daily, they would send tiny green shoots up to the skies, more every time Jill checked them. No amount of staring and pestering would speed up the emergence of the buds in the earth. Then, as if by magic, Jill would wake to find slender purple and yellow petals reaching up for her to admire. Such stunning colours blooming from onions. Just like a swan.

Nagging Iris to hurry up, Jill would proudly carry the tiny plants in her hands all the way to Southall, fiercely protecting them from poking siblings. To Jill, it didn't matter which grandmother she saw first on this occasion. It was more important to her that they hadn't been expecting a present and she was virtually bursting with excitement as she waited to see their faces aghast with surprise. Her dancing eyes sparkling a reflection into the happiness of the two special women. Shared tears borne of unpeeled onions and joy – and on her own special Mothering Saturday!

Then, eventually, came Easter. Bonnets made at Sunday school stood proudly on the heads of children belting out hymns about life and rebirth – more out of love for the tunes than the sentiment. Jill was no different and she wore her paper Easter Bonnet on several occasions when she visited her grandmothers. And, like all her friends and family, she looked forward to the Cadbury's eggs which seemed to multiply by day three, just when she had eaten enough chocolate to make the chicken which was to lay even more eggs.

Most of the eggs were the same. Crazy paved chocolate, hollow and carefully wrapped in the signature purple foil. Inside there would be single bags of chocolate buttons or maybe jelly tots which were not really big enough for sharing. Apart from the one which Jill was to receive... once.

Whilst visiting Maud, Edward's sister came to Maud's house and offered to treat all three grandchildren to an Easter egg. Not having any children of her own, she enjoyed treating them. Jill followed them all to Brophy's sweet shop, a short walk along the road. Once inside, the children were invited to choose an egg. Kenny chose a chocolate button one whilst Terry placed a jelly tot one on the counter. This left Jill to make her choice. Silently, she scoured the shelves for just the right one. She wanted something different from her brothers, something which was clearly just for her and very special. High up on the top shelf, she saw it, knowing this was her egg. The ladder creaked as Mr Brophy climbed up and lifted the basket down, complete with rustling cellophane and shiny bows! There was indeed an egg inside. A huge egg which was probably made for sharing. A heavy egg which weighed down her brothers as they struggled to carry it back to Maud's house. An even heavier egg when they had to promptly return it to Mr Brophy – unopened and unshared! Maud did not approve of such a waste of money on something so hollow – so back it went.

It didn't seem to matter to Jill that she had to wait a whole month until her birthday as it was always a time filled with fun, frivolity, cake and candles. She wasn't too keen on the cake part but suffered it in return for the presents she was given. This was also a time when her grandmothers would come to her house, all the way from Southall, just to see her! With her crocheted shopping bag bursting with a new party dress, fashioned by hand, Maud would arrive and immediately set her hands to work in the kitchen. Sandwiches and cakes competing for a space on the table. Shortly after, Ivy would amble in with a bag full to the brim with hustle and bustle – and maybe a hand-knitted jumper or an Enid Blyton book. Just when parties stopped meaning garden races, blind man's bluff and plates of iced gems, Jill couldn't be sure, but they filled *her* to the brim with a mosaic of memories for a long, long time to come.

The rest of the year rumbled from summer holidays, new school uniforms and pencil cases to the plaited loaves of Harvest Festival and the hollowed pumpkins of Halloween. Jill embraced the blustery autumn days as the leaves fell as if to make way for the snow to fall again in the winter.

Opening up chasms in their boughs so that the moon, working over-time, could light the way for Jack Frost to come out of retirement along with Father Christmas. How thoughtful of them.

Christmases in Maud's and Ivy's houses were scarily similar, it seemed to Jill. This was the only time that she felt and saw that both women had the same job to do. They had to make cakes almost black with fruit hidden inside a crusty shell of white icing. Glass trifle dishes were freshly washed until sparkling rainbows danced across the ceiling above them. Table cloths appeared from the same mysterious caverns as the glass baubles on the Christmas trees. Somehow Jill knew this was how they could find space to store the extra presents which Father Christmas couldn't fit into his sleigh. She sometimes felt quite sorry for him as there wasn't much space in her own house so her parents couldn't help him out. They just had to make sure the house was tidy so that, when he came down her chimney, he didn't trip over shoes or Lego as he placed their presents in three separate piles.

Jill's year was rounded off with the pleasures and pains of celebrating New Year's Eve. Mostly she would be at home and sleep in her own tiny bed but, as a small child, the most memorable nights were to be spent with Maud. After the usual tea of cold turkey and bubble and squeak, she didn't have to climb up the stairs to bed. Maud would delay placing the hot water bottle between the sheets and postpone nestling the china pot beneath the creaky bed until way, way after her usual bedtime. With stories of her own child-hood, Maud would compete with the sleep which was slowly overwhelming Jill in an attempt to keep her awake just one more minute. Under normal circumstances Maud would have ensured Jill was washed and tucked up in bed shortly after her tea. But for one evening in the whole year she indulged her grandchildren and treated them to a midnight. They weren't staying awake to raise a glass of peach wine or sing Auld Langsyne at midnight. Jill wouldn't have been able to take part in either but she had been told about "something just as special" happening in Dudley Road.

Wrapped up in crocheted blankets, cold noses turning red, Maud herded the children onto the front doorstep and waited. Hugging Jill close, she whispered words of encouragement to be still and quiet. The darkness which surrounded the glow of the streetlights reached down and silenced Jill's beating heart as she held her breath in anticipation. The clock started to chime in the background of the sitting room. Fighting the urge to count down to midnight, in case it stopped before she reached twelve, she glanced up at Maud. With one finger poised in the night air, she created an atmosphere saved from the danger of the darkness by the keenness of her hearing. And then it happened. On the strike of twelve, she heard a faint cracking sound seeking her out from the direction of the railway track. One short sound in one short moment.

Was the treat remarkable because she had been deemed old enough to hear the crack of pennies being crushed under the wheels of the train as it hurtled over the bridge at the end of the street? Or was it being able to stay up late enough to be swept inside Maud's night-time blanket, safer, softer and warmer than even her own little bed at home?

It wasn't until her teenage years that Jill spent New Year's Eve in Ivy's house. In a bedroom flooded with moonlight, dark corners small but big enough to harbour fears enough to prevent any girl from venturing out of bed until morning. Sounds of revellers coming from the street below did little to drown out the strange creaking noises in the rooms below. Not even Jill's vivid imagination could lift her from the bed to the comfort of the sitting room. She was to fall reluctantly into slumber imaging Ivy, sitting on the little settee with stew and dumplings for company.

Jill was in her teens when Ivy and Maud both passed away. Copious numbers of black and white photographs became strewn across the tables, once so gaily coloured. The blue of Ivy's Formica table complementing her bright eyes, hidden. The vibrant tablecloth on Maud's table complimenting the delicate flowers in her garden, obscured. Jill's crying eyes scoured the monochrome displays, looking for something momentous. Even the more recent colour photographs, of smiling children, with smiling adults didn't offer much comfort. There were two pictures which did reach out to her grieving heart, though. One, an old black and white photograph of Maud and Great Uncle Tom when they were obviously in their Sunday best. Complete with buttoned boots and a sash.

The other photograph was, again, a monochrome example of closeness. A ten-year-old Jill sat arm-in-arm with Ivy on a tiny settee. They were both beaming into the camera, Jill's own Polaroid camera as Iris took the picture.

This was probably the first time that Jill came to appreciate the wonder of the camera. Capturing a single moment in time which would bridge the generation gaps for years to come. Preserving the uniqueness of a scene which becomes part of a whole epic film, rerun in a kaleidoscope of memories. A photograph of one scene which is perceived in so many different ways by so many different people. Measuring just 2 inches wide, tattooed onto the mind.

Just two short years apart, both Maud and Ivy had passed away, leaving Jill bereft at the loss of two special women. Almost equal to the pain of bereavement was the loss of her link to her grandparents and the history they represented. Although Edward had passed away when Jill was a small child of seven years old her memories of him were distant but dear. He had called her "Toffee Nose" as she sat on his lap, by the fire in Dudley Road. As she got older, she remembered how he told her stories, although she couldn't recall which stories they had been. What she did remember, however, was the very day he died.

Iris and Richard had come and taken her from school in the middle of the day, which was odd in itself. Then they had driven to Southall on a week-day, also strange, but the starkest memory of all was when she arrived at her Grandmother's house. The adults were whispering and there was no sign of her Grandad. There were people in the garden talking so quietly that her brothers had told her to be quiet whilst they listened from the confines of the scullery. Even the front parlour had people in it so she had thought maybe there was to be another family party and the grown-ups were planning it, ever so quietly.

Nothing could prepare Jill for the sight which met her as she tiptoed into the darkened room. Kenny and Terry had told her that *she* was allowed in, despite the curtains being drawn, to see what was happening. Silently stepping silently onto the grey carpet, she caught a glimpse of someone lying down on a bed, behind a screen. There was somebody else kneeling beside the bed with their head bent forwards and it took a few seconds for Jill to recognise him as her dad. Within moments, she saw that it was her beloved Grandad lying in the bed and he wasn't moving, he was still and pale. She had just enough time to creep backwards, out of the room, before her dad turned away – relieved that the children hadn't seen his own father "laid out" in the front room. This memory was to stay with her forever. Whilst it had frightened her as a small girl, in a bizarre way, it hadn't haunted her as she reached adulthood. It was to become something of a treasured memory.

It was hers, the boys hadn't seen it and they couldn't claim the experience as theirs. It wasn't second hand and that was to give her immeasurable comfort in later years.

Four Leaf Clover

9   JILL – THE WOMAN.

Of course, there were to be more events which shaped her as a woman. It was true that she had inherited Maud's dark brown eyes and even Ivy's wherewithal to rustle up a hearty meal out of thin air. There was no doubt that Iris' traditions of tuna and tomato sandwiches eaten on a long journey, and the necessity of buying new clothes for a holiday had been passed down to her as well – regardless of budget. For Jill, it was the home-making skills which she valued most. Maud and Iris had both ensured that she could knit and sew. Even though it manifested in differing ways. Jill could fashion a blouse from a discarded dress; alter trousers or skirts for growing off spring; create dressing-up clothes from lace curtains and cushion covers, just like Maud. In the same vein, Jill could use a sewing machine with confidence; make a bed with hospital corners, which was not to be disturbed until night-time; hang net curtains which remained immaculate, simply because nobody dared to touch their poker straight gathering, just like Iris – all without the use of a spirit level!

Ivy had nurtured her ability to care for and comfort her cousins – mainly on a Saturday. These were the endearing qualities of two generations of women in her family and Jill was more than conscious of the importance of each and every one. It hadn't escaped her perceptive nature that both grandmothers had faced struggles – albeit of differing makings – and had developed resilience which had seen them through some extremely testing times.

Ivy had never heard a word from Jonny since the day he left. This was a regret of hers which she knew she couldn't rectify in her own lifetime. However it was partially explored by Iris long after her own children had grown up. Thankful for the scant snippets of detail about her father, Iris located him, met him and moved on. Leaving a gulf of sadness and indifference.

Likewise, Maud had never had another child which wasn't a regret, as such, as she indulged her grand-daughter in the way she might have if she and Edward had been mindful enough to have another baby – especially a daughter. In the same vein, Iris had overcome the difficulties associated with being Henry's step-daughter and worked relentlessly to be the mother she was determined (and destined) to be.

Jill wondered when she would be lucky enough to find her supply of resilience. Would it be the countless times she had her heart broken by a boyfriend? Would it be facing the sudden loss of Ivy two days before her sixteenth birthday? Would it be from the countless times she was returned to school, by the Welfare Woman, as she had vehemently hated virtually every day of her school life? The fact that all of these experiences and more, were already forming her own style of resilience eluded Jill. It wasn't as a teenager, but as a mother when she would need her reserves – and more - to achieve her own goal of being the best mum she could be.

Having trained as a Nursery Nurse, Jill had already made a conscious decision to apply her newly acquired child-care skills to being a mum. To her, it seemed a natural progression from college, to a job as a nanny and then rounding it up with being a mum. Although she wasn't in a hurry to start a family of her own, she did have plans to marry Stuart, a friend of her aunt's, and to move into a flat which was owned by Richard. Their romance had started with a kind of blind date, her aunt playing Cupid. But it was Iris who held her head as she vomited in the taxi earlier in the day, nerves and excitement overwhelming her.

Never the less, Jill met him on the station bridge, in Hayes, before going ice skating in Richmond. Stuart paid for her bus fare, entry to the ice rink and for her Pernod and lemonade in the pub after. This "chivalry" wasn't wasted on her and she was very soon head over heels in love with him. They weren't quite inseparable as he moved to Hampshire a few month later but Jill would travel to see him every other weekend. Making the most of her baby face, the smitten Jill would buy a child's ticket and daydream for the entire two-hour coach journey.

Arriving just as Stuart finished work for the week, they would meet in the town, spend the evening and the contents of his wage packet in the pub, swinging by the Chinese take-away on the way home. Jill loved these weekends which were paving the way for them to spend the rest of their lives together. Crazy-paving welcomed Stuart into Richard's and Iris's home as he moved in with them to be nearer to her. Jill thought the icing really was on her cake when Stuart bought her a tiny black guinea pig. No cage, no food, just a furry bundle which she called Satan — for some reason.
Two years of energy, fun and tears were to follow. A holiday in Yorkshire, visits to his Nan's house for a roast, New Year's Eve with his dad, swimming in Hayes pool, all melded together.

Before too long, Stuart's proposal saw Jill proudly wearing Maud's diamond engagement ring, still as sparkly as it was in 1930.
As Jill studied at college and Stuart found work locally, plans for their future were being made. Having already carved out a career path, which would round nicely into mother hood, Jill was in her element as she costed out her potential earnings as a nanny. Coupled with Stuart's wages, they were going to be in position to rent their own place within a year of their marriage. In fact, the future looked even rosier than she had originally thought. Richard and Iris had decided to move to Berkshire just after Jill finished college, buying a huge Victorian house with two self-contained flats, one of which would be for Jill and Stuart to live in. A perfect start to their impending marriage in the August.

However, fact being stronger than fiction, Jill did move into the flat but without Stuart. It seemed that, as the wedding grew nearer his commitment to her grew further away. All the way back to the safety of his dad's house! It was just a few short weeks later that a heartbroken Jill watched through brilliant white net curtains while her parents calmly handed Stuart's parents a box of his tricks. No, she knew that he wasn't a member of the Magic Circle but he must have been some kind of magician though. Sleight of hand concealed not only his fears from her view, but sliced up her future with swords of steel before whisking it away in a puff of smoke. Leaving her a black guinea pig instead of a white rabbit. No top hat. And so as she sat, heartbroken at the shattering of her hopes and dreams, Jill's resilience came and went – just like Stuart.

It was 1980 and a young woman with her own flat was too good a chance to pass by for Nigel. Whilst it was Jill who made the first move in a local pub, Nigel was more than keen to see her flat and, within a very short time he had moved in his collection of black bags and boxes. In years to come, Jill would still admit that she found him extremely handsome and his public school voice only added to the attraction. Jill had the family trait of being attracted to a smooth talker, not sure where it came from. She knew that Ivy had fallen for the suave and sophistication of Jonny, only to face the reality of his shyness of responsibility. With Iris and Richard, on the other hand, it had been love at first sight, and second sight and third sight…. The fact that Nigel had been thrown out of his parent's house, and was without a permanent address, had influenced the decision for him to move in but Jill convinced herself it was meant to be. Her heart was slowly emerging from the darkness left by Stuart, into the light which seemed to illuminate the halo she thought she saw above Nigel's head. Finding space for his meagre belongings in the flat was a lot easier than she had thought.

Like millions of women before her, Jill's relationships weren't without its' fair share of trials and tribulations. Nigel made no secret of the fact that he preferred the pub to the pulpit, or that his love of the Rolling Stones was second to none, only just a notch above the love he had for himself. However, Jill was deeply in love with him and continued to accept him, warts and all, for who he was. Whilst he didn't actually have any warts, Nigel had plans which didn't always include her. One being him deciding to hitch a lift to the Midlands to visit an old school friend whilst the country was gripped by the most treacherous snow storm since 1963. With news channels warning of life-threatening snow fall and rescuing tractors being stuck in ditches, Jill worried all the while he was away. True Nigel style, he hadn't left her an address or contact number. It was a waiting game as to when he was going to return and she spent at least one entire night with the telephone cord wrapped around her hand in case he called. He didn't.

Compared to Jill's handful of friends, his social circle also seemed rather "alternative". Most of them were older than Nigel, some working and some unemployed. Brothers of friend's home from Unit for the summer congregated with sisters of friends, also home from Uni. Not all of them would return at the end of the summer, however, choosing instead to take a year out and learn to play an instrument or how to speak Mandarin Chinese. Others travelling the world "to find themselves". Jill found this one a bit confusing because, in her experience, wherever she went she was there! Not rocket science. Also, several of them were linked by birth or a school brotherhood, and seemed to have known each other forever. Either way, they certainly knew how to throw some raucous parties.

One New Years' Eve the whole eclectic posse went to a fancy dress pub crawl in a nearby village. Dressed up to the nines, they both entered into the spirit of things, even when a beer fight broke out and copious amounts of London Pride bitter were sprayed across the room (probably only to add to the musty smell of hops which mounted year after year). With only two pubs in the village, a decision was made to do a chain the Conga from one to the other. They sang and snaked across the village, diverting only for a quick "lap" of the bistro which faced the green. Diners amused and bemused. Waiters dodging them with carefully balanced trays of hors d'oeuvres.

Despite these high jinks, the mood was to turn sour for Jill. It was following the beer fight, as midnight approached, that the patrons of the second pub started to prepare for a hearty round of Auld Langsyne. Congregated in the middle of the public bar and forming a rather fluid "circle" of drunken revellers, the preparation for New Year kisses began. Unknown to Jill, the revellers included Danielle, an old girlfriend of Nigel's who had joined the group. She just blended in with the crowd, laughing and leaning in closely to shout a compliment or something into an ear, vying with the ever-increasing volume of the music. As the singing reached a crescendo of merriment, Jill found herself being ushered away from the swaying circle. As the countdown reached midnight, she pushed her way back into the centre and soon came face to face with Nigel. He might have closed his eyes and ears to the melee which surrounded them, and drew close for a New Year kiss. But it was with Danielle and not Jill! Calm and resolute, with a determination stronger than the ale which flowed across the floor, Jill asked Nigel for the door key. Then she simply turned on her beer-soaked heels and marched out of the pub. With her head held high, Jill faced the swirling snow and glistening ice alone as she walked the three miles home.

Bearing no resemblance to any midnight she had had before, Jill found herself marching in defiance, with the thought of a nice dry bed to fall into. Glimmers of a distant memory which captured her standing, cold and tired one particular midnight flitted in and out of her mind. Someone was there to keep her safe and guide her into bed as the neighbours wished each other Happy New Year, Walton style. Try as she might, Jill couldn't quite place the person or location but, never the less, she was guided safely home to bed.

Nestled inside the freezing snowdrifts was something she was yearning for…her first taste of resilience.

Despite his blatant display of infidelity, Jill continued to love Nigel and they soon made up – with the help of his friends and the disappearance of Danielle. In fact, Jill was elated beyond her imagination to find herself pregnant in the spring of 1983. Indeed, having worked for a while as a daily nanny, at just twenty years old she was to become a mum and all seemed rosy for Jill and Nigel. They hurriedly made wedding plans although, with hindsight, Jill had to admit that this was mainly due to her being pregnant and not wanting her baby to have a different surname than her. Still, at the same time, she genuinely believed they had all they needed – a roof over their heads, a baby on the way and a love which would conquer all.

With a waistline which was rapidly turning into a coast line, Jill wasn't going to be wed in the same tailored suit as Iris (even if she had kept it for all those years). It came as no surprise that Iris immediately came to the rescue by getting her sewing skills into action. Jill had watched her mum thread her sewing machine needle and adjust the tension maybe a thousand times or more. The times she sat in awe of how Iris made the delicate threads weave into intricate rows, exactly where she wanted them. But this time it was different. This time Jill noticed the happiness and pride in her mum's eyes as she worked her magic. She could have been a human pin cushion herself, for all she cared, she just wanted to make her little girl look ever the blushing bride and radiant mum-to-be all at once.

With a flowing bodice and lacy sleeves, the dress actually complimented her bump and Jill secretly wondered if the colour was a sign – it was baby blue.

This added to the ensuing speculation about whether the baby would be a girl or a boy and names were chosen in preparation for either. A ring on thread suspended over her rounding belly confirmed she was carrying a girl when it span in clockwise circles. Craving salty and savoury food confirmed Jill was going to give birth to a boy. However, one of Jill's aunts had more than an old wives' tale for a prediction, which had quite a profound effect on Jill.

Apparently, her aunt had been waiting for a train in her home town, which was at least a hundred miles from where Jill and Nigel lived. As she waited, a total stranger approached her and said that she felt an overwhelming need to tell her about her niece – who was expecting. The woman went on to say that her niece was having a few health problems with her pregnancy but that she would have a healthy baby girl and name her Louise. In an attempt to keep this prediction a secret from Jill, her aunt chose to whisper the story to another aunt, as the wedding photos were being taken. However, deafness wouldn't hinder Jill's life for another three decades yet and she heard every little word.

Determined that the stranger had wrongly predicted the gender, Jill virtually willed her unborn baby to be a boy. In reality, she didn't mind what the sex was, she just wanted a healthy bouncing baby to love. Even as she went into labour she was still convincing herself that her baby would be a boy and they would name him James Austin Jones.

Four Leaf Clover

10   JILL – THE MOTHER

Iris and Richard were overjoyed at the arrival of their first grandchild one Saturday afternoon in September. Like a stunning blend of at least three generations of women, Verity was the apple of her parents' (and grandparents') eyes. Maud's brown eyes shone against Ivy's flawless complexion; framed by downy hair which delicately curved into Iris's widows peak; Jill's rosebud mouth beneath the petals of Verity's own perfect button of a nose. To Jill, she was perfect in every way. Apart from being a girl and, therefore, couldn't be named James! Thankfully, they had chosen a girls' name too so she was soon registered as Verity Jones. Simple, but Jill felt their baby was so perfect that she didn't need a middle name.

Like her mum and grandmothers before her, motherhood was the making of Jill and there was no mistaking who she took after with her own baby. All of them! She cuddled Verity as much as she wanted – even though the ward midwife chastised her for "cuddling baby too much". Verity's response was to state that Verity wasn't "baby", she was her daughter and she would cuddle her if and when she wanted! Likewise, she would make her own decisions about when, where and if she wanted to breastfeed Verity. Sometimes Jill wondered if the nurses had delivered 7lb and 5 ounces of stubbornness with the baby, or if this was something all mums felt? Maybe she was absent from college the day they taught that one?

When the time came for Jill and Nigel to take their new born baby home it made perfect sense to Iris that Verity should be dressed in a matinee jacket, booties and bonnet which she had lovingly knitted, in mint green.

Anything else wouldn't have been good enough for this little darling, and Jill agreed. Swaddled in the matching shawl, Jill lay her on the hospital bed and took time to drink in the sight. Verity sleeping in her own, brand new layette made from a knitting pattern some twenty-eight years old.

True to form, as soon as the news of the baby's arrival reached him, Richard had hurried to the shop and bought a plush teddy bear. With thick white fur and big brown eyes it resembled a baby seal and Richard thought it was the perfect gift. But it didn't even come close to the love he felt for the gift of Verity.

Arriving home, Jill and Nigel were unprepared for the sight of a beautiful wooden crib which Iris and Richard had bought. With a pink blanket as soft as gossamer lying across sheets woven by snow angels it was a perfect little nest for Verity to sleep in. And she really loved to sleep. They couldn't have wished for a more content baby who looked like a delicate china doll. Rosy cheeks were even more exaggerated by the white brushed cotton gowns which had belonged to her uncles. It might have been sewn and embroidered almost thirty years ago but Jill thought nothing of slipping it over Verity's head as homage to her own grandmother. Three little ducks stepping across the bodice, so minute they must have been embroidered by fairies as they in turn danced across. Softening the fabric with every step, sifting their precious fairy dust into each stitch.

Grandparents featured high on the list of Verity's fans as they would vie for the prize position of pushing her along in her Silver Cross pram. Whilst Iris had wanted her first grandchild to have everything new, she was in agreement that her daughter would live within her means. This meant that the majority of baby clothes and equipment were either bought from the local charity shops or donated by friends whose' children no longer needed them. As with the arrival of any new baby, friends and family visited with gifts of pink knitted dresses or stripy baby-grows. Aunts made beautiful dresses in forest green velvet and some in pretty floral prints which were complimented by the feather light matinee jackets and cardigans. All unique outfits which leaned themselves well to the fresh fragrances of fabric conditioner and baby shampoo.

What was more important to Iris and Richard was that Verity had somewhere new to sleep and this is what prompted Richard to make the most stunning cot for his beautiful grand-daughter. Each part was so carefully crafted with bars of oak and a frame of teak, turned and polished by his own fair hands. Perfect dovetails and brass screws safely secured joins. As Richard completed this masterpiece, expertly applying layer upon layer of French polish and teak oil, Iris waited patiently in the wings to add her own finishing touches. Ever so carefully, she placed the white lace drapes over the bars, teasing them into ruffles, as only Iris could. Long white satin bows secured them. Dazzling Broderie-Anglaise, quilted blankets turned back at the corners, ready and waiting for a cherished angel of a baby. Her very own blankety-bed.

As Jill lay her daughter gently against the soft, white sheets she felt her heart melting, overwhelmed with pride. She heard the gentle and subtle murmurs. She smelled the unique sweet earthiness of a new born. She saw the softest, pink cheeks of her baby. A moment which, although seen through eyes misted with tears, born of undying love and devotion, was to be eternally etched in the swelling hearts of her parents and grandparents. Richard's silent tears made way for something else – the realisation that he was witnessing the moment when the lives of his wonderful women had changed. Dovetailed together, bonded forever.

Verity grew into the happiest baby, earning a nick-name of "Smiler". She also had a very healthy appetite which would definitely have attracted the attention of her great grandmothers. Whilst Maud may have been somewhat alarmed at how much food one baby could eat, Ivy would have taken great pride in the way she tried (and enjoyed) such a wide range of foods, especially home-cooked stews. Good ham and beetroot was to earn its place sometime later.

When Jill had initially discovered she was pregnant, Nigel accepted that he was going to have to start earning as money had been virtually non-existent since they had started to live together. Although this shaped the way she had been budgeting, Jill was finding it increasingly difficult to juggle being a mother and a home-maker. There was a limit to what meals she could rustle up with onions, tinned tomatoes, egg noodles and green beans. So it was a huge relief when Nigel found a "proper job" and brought in a reasonable wage. Things were still tight but improving slowly. Jill might have still been struggling to put appealing and nourishing meals on the table, but it was Iris who invariably came to the rescue. With a keen eye for a bargain, Iris would maximise on any supermarket offering the trendy "buy one, get one free" items. On more than one occasion, the "one free" miraculously bypassed Iris's larder, ending up in Jill's cupboard.

So, on Richard's payday, as opposed the Nigel's, Jill would do her best to cook something cheap and tasty, which could be blended for Verity to eat at a later stage. As a new mum, it was important to her to prepare fresh food for her growing baby. Although tinned baby food was comparatively expensive, Jill preferred to feed Verity home-cooked foods. At college she had learned the nutritional value of different foods and had made a vow to cook from scratch when she had her own baby. Of course, this extended to meals they ate with Iris and Richard too.

Jars of baby food had occasionally been part of Jill's own diet, as a baby. Mainly for convenience when they were out for the day, or if at a friend's house, it was warmed to a safe temperature and spooned into Jill's waiting mouth. No fuss, no waste. In fact, Jill could sometimes still be found eating the tiny portions, as an adult. Her guilty pleasure.

It was for convenience that Jill provided her parents with a jar of yummy Heinz Lamb Dinner, when she and Nigel went out one evening. With motherly love turning into "motherly missing my baby love" Jill arrived home a lot earlier than expected. Verity grumped and gurned in the lounge whilst her lunch was being prepared, but not quick enough for her liking. As Jill walked into the kitchen, she found Richard standing by the gas cooker with a puzzled look on his face. In one hand he held the small jar. In the other hand he held a small saucepan. His problem, he said, was that he couldn't remember if he needed to remove the jar lid before he immersed it in the saucepan of boiling water. Puzzlement jumped to Jill's face, quickly chased away by the realisation that her dad, a highly intelligent engineer, didn't know how to reheat baby food. Even *she* knew that if he didn't open the sealed jar before boiling it in water it would open itself – rapidly! Now seemed like the perfect time to introduce Richard to the microwave! As she acknowledged this simple example of the generation gap, Jill thanked her lucky stars that she hadn't asked him to wash any nappies as she occasionally used disposable ones!

Jill welcomed these opportunities to "educate" her dad about modern day parenting. If only Nigel wanted to learn so much about his daughter. It wasn't that he ignored her – quite the opposite. He never passed by a chance to help her improve her muscle tone. Jill would watch, with her heart in her mouth, as Nigel swung Verity into the air and, thankfully, caught her again. However, it was when they were alone with their daughter that Nigel showed his genuine love and affection. Jill sometimes found herself getting hung up on seeing that Verity met her development milestones. Every day she would read baby alphabet books to her, tell her the names of every colour on the beautiful new clothes that she wore. And so it went on. Even Verity's toys were leaning towards educational props.

Although Nigel preferred to engage in more raucous play than Jill, he could often be found playing with the hippo shape sorter. Even when Verity was asleep, Nigel and his friends would have a competition so see who could get all eight pieces of plastic inside the hippo in the shortest time. Jill found it amusing but thought it was a bit excessive to see that they had introduced rules. She watched on in amazement as the grown men lined up the various shapes and raced to put them the corresponding holes – in a particular colour order. Using strategies which were also applied to the games of Risk they regularly played.

During the late-night games sessions, it wasn't unheard of for the noise to rise to the crescendo of roaring laughter. Jill often took herself in to the bedroom as cries of "nearly" and "cheat" seeped through the thick basement walls. The sounds of competitor and peacemaker were somewhat soothing for her. She enjoyed hearing the round of belly laughs. What wasn't so welcome were the orders which came through the walls for sustenance. It was obviously thirsty work, putting shapes into hippos, and they really worked up an appetite too. Maybe once or twice Jill was more than happy to take in cans of beer. Even providing a late-night snack of scrambled eggs and rissoles wasn't a problem. As the hours ticked by she began to resent having to keep the kitchen "open". Like her cherub in the other bedroom, Jill longed for sleep on such nights. Or maybe a little bit of appreciation for her efforts.

Eventually, the day came when Jill had had her fill. It was on a Thursday, Nigel was going to work later, following a dental appointment. Prior to his going out, he had told her that he needed his shoes cleaning before he went to work, and the task fell to Jill. Evidently, Nigel had probably planned to pay the dentist with his dwindling supply of manners. Following this, he was going to have to rush in order to catch the next bus to work. He needed a sandwich to eat on the journey.

Whilst her husband was opening his mouth wide, at one end of town, Jill was opening the cling film at the other end. Wrapping it tightly around a cheese and tomato sandwich, Jill smiled. How pleased Nigel would be when he saw his shiny brogues. How pleased he would be when he ate his lunch on the packed bus, ensuring he wasn't too late for work. Such a dutiful wife must surely be appreciated?

Within the hour, Nigel breezed in, grabbed his polished and packaged things and breezed out. Jill could be fairly sure that he would stride out to the bus garage, instead of running, to look every bit the businessman. Jill was absolutely certain that he would attempt to discreetly unwrap the cling film, not wanting to attract attention. These were the "givens" of Nigel's character. Jill could also guarantee that he would be mortified as he sank his newly polished teeth into the sandwich. The familiar taste of the hygienist's toothpaste would be lingering, ready to mingle with that of bread and cheese. The bus would be full to the brim with shoppers and grisly babies. Nigel would be ravenous.

In fact, Nigel was so hungry that he decided to eat his lunch as soon as he got on the bus — at the start of the hour-long journey. With crumbs and confusion on his face, this businessman bit into the bread, into the cheese and struggled to bite through the tomato. As he drew the food away from his mouth the offending slice seemed to stretch and wind around his tongue like a boa constrictor. Becoming more taut and tangled the more he pulled, it was the other passengers who recognised the grey knots before Nigel. Grey knots of string, clogged with slimy lumps of partly chewed cheese. Yellow blobs, like Magician's handkerchiefs, bobbing between face and fingers. Inches of string seeming more like yards, to an extremely embarrassed and "mortified" Businessman! Jill got no thanks.

Whilst Jill flourished as a mum, Nigel was finding it extremely difficult to settle down into being the dutiful husband and doting father. Try a she might, Jill couldn't fathom out a way to include him more in Verity's care without making him feel burdened. Maybe it was because he didn't come from such a close and inclusive family? Or maybe because Nigel had ambitions which were becoming further out of his reach, the more time he spent with Jill? Her fuddled mind was still trying right to fathom it out right up to the day when Nigel dropped the biggest bombshell ever. Over lunch, in what she called "the New Year's Eve" pub, he calmly told her that he wanted to separate, just before he ordered his cheeseburger and chips.

The lure of life in the city was too much to bare for Nigel and it was only a matter of time before Jill found herself a lone parent. The roles of mummy and daddy intertwining. Not quite a matriarch, nor a patriarch Jill was a "Natriarch", without any money and with little prospect of climbing out of the rut. By all intents and purposes it seemed that simple. He wasn't happy with her, Jill was happy with being a mother and their commitment to each other had just evaporated into the toxic suburban air.

Jill was devastated as she had no idea that this was on the cards. Throughout her teenage years, there had been boyfriends who had cruelly broken her heart and simply walked away. Deep down Jill knew that she had to find a way to cope without him. A way to raise Verity on her own. With Iris as her mother, she wasn't really on her own. Together they would share the responsibility of bringing her up to the absolute best they possibly could. Neither of them had experience of being a single parent but it didn't take too long for just the right dose of resilience to shine through the autumn gloom.
Nigel was to satisfy his yearning for travelling to exotic and far flung places. Maybe even Jersey?
Verity continued to be Jill's main and only focus. It was true that Nigel had left her the furniture in the flat she still rented from her father, but this wasn't going to keep her company or provide a secure future for Verity. Jill became increasingly reliant on the skills she had picked up from being Iris' daughter. Using cheaper foods, she invented "in-a-pot" which consisted of a stew of tinned vegetables and a small can of corned beef. What it lacked in nutrients was made up for in taste and it never tasted the same twice. Concocting her own version of one of her favourite dishes became a regular occurrence and, as she grew older, it became a favourite of Verity's too.

Eventually the time came for Jill and Verity to move into their own home, a short distance from Iris and Richard. Although not too far away, Jill still needed to get to their house by bus to join Iris for a shopping trip into town or to visit for the traditional Sunday roast. This was the highlight of her week as her mums' roast potatoes were second to none and she always managed to come away with a little doggy bag of chicken and potatoes. Whilst Jill could only afford to cook a roast occasionally she still kept the menu for her and Verity as varied as her money would allow. They came to look forward to having "pick and mix" which bore no resemblance to the sweets laid out in Woolworths. For this culinary delight, they would sort through the freezer and take out all of the half-finished packets of burgers, sausages and fish fingers and cook them all together with a side dish of tinned tomatoes. "Make do" was to become a bit of a mantra for Jill for some time to come.

Life wasn't all scrimping and scraping though. There were times when Jill managed to save up for holidays and treats, although she couldn't have done it without the considerable help of her parents. If it wasn't for Iris giving her the spare item from a "buy one, get one free" offer things would have been very different for her, as a mother. Like her parents, Jill knew the value of a holiday for children (and herself) so she made a concerted effort to plan for at least one break a year. Occasionally it would mean a short stay with an aunt, or cousin, but there were also holidays which took them far and wide. Wherever they went, Jill was determined to make it as memorable for Verity as her own childhood holidays. Right down to the tuna sandwiches.

By booking the hotel as early in the season as possible, Iris, Jill, Richard and Verity all travelled to the Amalfi Coast in Italy. It came as no surprise to the adults that Verity rushed into the bedroom and quickly changed into her new "holiday dress" as soon as they arrived. Relaxing after the flight was instantly shelved as Verity paraded around the hotel disco, swishing her skirt and grooving to Italian music. The luxury of eating huge pizzas with squid on top and being able to choose from ten different ice-cream flavours seemed to pass her by and came naturally. Taking everything in her stride in this way, both impressed and surprised them all. The way Verity skipped her way through the holiday, carefree and innocent, was a priceless "one free" gift. This was to be the first of many trips abroad for Verity, albeit in years to come. There was no doubt in Jill's mind, as she watched her daughter laugh and frolic in the pool, that Verity was soaking up the memorable experience as much as the sun.

As a typical Taurean, being happiest in a relationship, eventually Jill found herself in a new relationship and ready to commit to spending the rest of her life with Phil. They had met via a mutual friend and she (not so secretly) fancied him, even though she was going out with another man at the time. So it seemed natural to Jill that, when that relationship ended she should start another one with Phil. He wasn't particularly tall but he was handsome and had the same brown eyes as her. There were other attributes which attracted Jill to him, least of all the car he drove and the fact that he seemed to know of many lovely places to take her. It may have seemed shallow that Jill was impressed by Phil's car, with its' soft leather seats, but it was a far cry from the used and abused estate car she drove. His car was a calming off-white colour and the leather on the seats extended to the short gear knob. A walnut dashboard gleamed as it reflected Phil's boyish looks. With mats covering worn nylon carpet, instead of the plush brown twist of Phil's care, Jill appreciated her car all the same. It had been the only car she could afford, previously owned by her mum, but it was perfect for getting Verity to and from school in Eton. Every morning the matt orange beast trundled into the quiet lanes of the prestigious college. Waking and shaking the pupils into their gowns, it would offer a little splutter in an attempt at "clearing One's throat". Finally, Jill would carefully squeak and squeeze it into a space near the school and walk, with her head held high, purposefully into the playground.

Phil worked locally and would regularly finish early enough to spend time with Jill before Verity went to bed. They were soon inseparable. They cooked their favourite meals together (from real ingredients – not a pick and mix). There were days out to Thorpe Park, lazy picnics in Henley-on-Thames and a camping trip to Wiltshire. The latter included visiting Jill's favourite aunt on the way home. Her aunt's approval of Phil was important for Jill and she was bowled over when her aunt described him as "Choochy", which she took to mean handsome and cute.

With the seal of approval from Iris, Richard and her beloved aunt, Jill wasted no further time before she proposed to Phil during another camping holiday to Wales. On the beach in Tenby, Verity looked on as Jill carefully built a small aeroplane of sand and wrote "will you marry me?" on one side. Several holiday makers walked past, smiling and looking at them expectantly. Eventually, Phil walked around and read the message. With no hesitation he quickly hugged Jill in acceptance before writing "yes" on the other side of the plane! Jill knew that Phil wasn't just going to be the rock on which she could build her future. He would be the sun on her skin, the wind in her hair and the sand between her toes.

Nigel was still very much a part of Verity's life but there was no hiding the fact that Phil had come to love her as his own. Committed to securing a healthy future for these two wonderful "women", Phil worked harder than ever. Devotion and love illuminated his face whenever he looked at them. To onlookers it was hard to tell whether it was Phil's, Verity's or Jill's laughter which infected them all as they grew closer and closer. With his prized camera, Phil would photograph them at every opportunity. Capturing the magical sparks which surrounded them. Creating indelible memories for the three of them. Providing a snapshot, frozen in time, for anyone who might shuffle through them in years to come.

The only blot on the horizon was how Iris seemed to be slightly mistrusting of Phil. Jill knew that this was due to the way she had learnt to distrust step-fathers in general. After all, Henry hadn't been the most upstanding example and the *only* example Iris had to refer to. However, a blind man could see just how far removed from each other the two men were. A deaf man could hear the beating of Phil's heart racing at the sheer mention of Jill's name. And you didn't need a lip-reader to know that the love between them was indubitable. True to Iris' warmth and generosity, every whisper of worry swept far away as she gave thanks that Jill had found happiness once again. A happiness which was to last.

On a blustery November day, Jill and Phil became husband and wife and couldn't have smiled so much, for so long as they did, as they took their vows. With family and friends watching lovingly on, Richard proudly walked his daughter down the aisle. Walking behind them, in tiny satin shoes, was Verity and two other very special bridesmaids. The fairy rings of pink and white roses set carefully on their heads complimented Jill's bouquet perfectly. Hearts melted and smiles grew wider as the congregation turned to watch three little angels taking twinkle steps, in stunning floral dresses – sewn lovingly by Iris.

The following twelve months saw the new little family growing from strength to strength. Sleepy Sunday mornings were intermingled with crazy cooking "evenings", when all three of them could be found eating different meals. Phil would add a dollop of mayonnaise beside his chicken Kiev. Jill opted for a squirt of brown sauce on her steak and kidney pie. Verity, invariably munched her way through a mountain of spaghetti Bolognese – topped with grated cheddar. This wasn't the feast fit for Kings but it reflected the nurturing of three individuals, with three different tastes, in unity.

In month thirteen, Tim arrived. With Phil by her side, Jill gave birth to their amazing son. Following quite a dramatic arrival, Tim was placed into his father's arms and a palpable bond was forged. An exhausted Jill watched on as Phil tenderly cradled his son in his arms. His dark brown eyes explored every soft curve of his son's face. Mesmerised by the brush strokes of his tiny mouth, downy hair on his smooth head, and ten pink nails dabbed neatly on the end of ten tiny fingers. A magical moment when Jill witnessed Love breathe life into Phil and Tim, simultaneously. Inhaling Fairy Dust, exhaling innocence.

Life as a new mother in 1991 was so far removed from the time Verity had arrived. Whether it was the way society had changed or their individual circumstances, life was easier for the couple. Although they could afford some new baby items, Jill chose to bring her son home from hospital in the same mint green knitted outfit which Verity had worn as she met the world. Somehow she didn't see it as a hand-me-down. It was more of a special heirloom, destined to be steeped in family history.

Verity took to the role of a big sister with the same excitement as she always did when gifts arrived in her lap. Being eight years older than this little new-comer, she was able to help with some of the baby "stuff". Equally, Verity was old and eloquent enough to say when she really didn't want to help. She was to bide her time until it became her self-appointed responsibility to teach him some of the ways of the World – her way.

Grandparents, however, weren't of the belief of biding their time. They knew life was short, babies weren't babies for long and grandchildren were there solely to be spoilt. This included Verity and Tim who were indulged to the extreme by both sets of grandparents, with toys and treats. As Jill sat and watched the unrivalled devotion manifest itself she caught the shortest glimpse of how she might one day be a Grandmother too. Maybe her lap would never be big enough to cuddle all of her future grandchildren and great grandchildren all at once, but there was no mistaking the fact that her heart was big enough to love them all for ever.

Tim was another placid baby who always woke with a smile. Instead of having his parents deep brown eyes he had "inherited" bright blue eyes and a mop of poker-straight blond hair. Sometimes Jill would marvel at this difference and sometimes she would try and will his eyes to darken, so that he resembled her and Phil more. Either way, he was beautiful and his blue eyes turned almost violet when she dressed him in pastel blue outfits which Phil's mum had bought.

Money was still a slight problem for the new parents but the baby and Verity kept them busy. Years before, when Verity was two years old, Jill had joined a local Methodist Church. The Minister was a Yorkshire man who enjoyed nothing better than a long discussion about all things religious – or not, as the case may be. It was Jill's pleasure to introduce him to Phil and didn't hesitate to ask him to perform their wedding ceremony. He gladly agreed and was even happier when he was asked to baptise Tim in the spring of 1992. The ceremony was special for several reasons but not least of all because Jill had a close relationship with the Minister. In fact, when he first saw Tim, he said that he was a special baby and he had been born into a loving and secure family. This meant so much to Jill.

Tim's' Baptism arrangements weren't without some tactful planning on Jill's part. Whilst Phil's mum doted on Tim she had an aversion to her grandchild having used or second-had clothes. Immaculately turned out herself, she only wanted the best for him, as grandparents do. In fact, the one pre-owned item she did want him to wear was a christening gown which had been worn by Phil and one of his cousins. Unfortunately, or otherwise, Tim was such a bonny baby that the lace gown didn't fit him by the time the Minister baptised him one Mothering Sunday in the following March. Instead he wore a brand new gown and cap, wrapped in the most intricate white cape, knitted by Iris. Even Phil's mum appreciated how resplendent he looked as she cuddled him alongside her own mother.

It wasn't a surprise when Jill and Phil invited the Minister to celebrate Tim's first birthday with them. What was a surprise, however, was the way Tim reacted in his own individual way when opening one of his presents. Phil had bought him a brightly coloured toy drill, complete with a hard plastic case to keep it in. It even made the rasping noise of a real electric drill. At the time they lived in a flat in Langley which had a long, narrow hall. Every night Phil would come home and place his own tools along one wall, as opposed to leaving them in his company van overnight. On more than one occasion, Phil accidentally walked into the tool boxes and said a few choice words.

At his birthday party, Tim ripped the paper off with enthusiasm. Then he calmly lined it up with Phil's tool boxes, in the hall. Not being happy with that, Tim stood still, kicked the toy drill and loudly repeated the very words that Phil had so often used! Shocked and embarrassed, Jill and Phil wanted the ground to open up beneath them. However, when they looked towards the Minister to apologise they saw that he was, in fact, stifling a giggle.

Now, at the ripe old age of fifty-four Jill was unusually calm. Sitting cocooned in a rather large, but beautiful, patchwork quilt Jill found herself reminiscing. The quilt had been hand-sewn by Verity; her belly was full of "in-a-pot"; her daughter was settling into her own home by arranging pink flamingo cushions on the sofa, and her arms were cuddling the first of her amazing grandchildren. Just how she had arrived in such a blissful position in her life wasn't important. The qualities and skills which had been nurtured by three such special women were the real treasures. Now seeing her daughter apply them as a young woman, and a mother, left Jill with an inner warmth which far outweighed that of the brightest star in Heaven.

Jill had no regrets about how she had been as a mother. She had tackled the challenges, enjoyed the rewards and been thankful for having been blessed with two incredible children. Seeing them blossom into young adults with their own set of skills, talents and values gave her immeasurable fulfilment. Jill's achievement evident in theirs. Knowing she had done her utmost to equip them for their own futures, no matter what this held.

This was the over-riding feeling which comforted and kept Jill sane when her beloved mum returned to join Ivy and Maud, in 2016. Nothing on Earth could have prepared her for the cataclysmic torrent of emotions which wracked her mind – and her heart. A cruel thief, stealing her precious mum as she slept, before her eyes. But a thief with a conscience, laying Iris in the path of Angels who led her safely home to Heaven. Jill's tears didn't fall freely that day. Absorbed by her knowledge that Iris hadn't feared Death, cotton wool grew heavier as time passed. When the vigilance of the fibres could take no more, her longings were swept away by fresh running water. The saltiness of sadness leaving trade-marks of grief in her eyes.

Yet, in moments of quiet, as she tenderly caressed the tiny gold cross which hung around her neck, Jill felt as if she was a tiny tile in a puzzle. Believing that one day, she didn't care when, it would be her turn to slide across and up into place. Settling beside Iris and her incredible grandmothers, she would be another part of the puzzle of Life. When the colours of her kaleidoscope settled.

As a woman, mother and grandmother, Iris had bestowed upon her the values of honesty, integrity, love and forgiveness. Try as Jill might, she couldn't comprehend the notion that these qualities had been "hand-me-downs". They had been the legacy of some remarkable women whom she had been proud to call her family. Now it was Verity who would come to nurture those qualities, for her own daughters and granddaughters.

It was at that exact moment that Jill realised that what you do or say to your children today could be their memories of tomorrow. Treasure every perfect moment with them, as they will, with you.

Four Leaf Clover

11   THE AUTHOR: A FINAL NOTE

Having been interested in her family history for most of her life, Jacquie Crowther found writing about the matriarchs who graced her with their skills and abilities extremely cathartic. For most of her adult life mental illness had accompanied Jacquie through some of her darkest of nights into her brightest days. Acting like a new-found therapy, writing and drawing empowered her to embrace the wonder of three remarkable women, *as well as* herself.

When her mother lost her own fight in Life, in 2016, a stubborn sadness hovered and loomed around her. As she wrote each chapter, reminiscing her way through bygone years, it lifted as if captured by the drawing in of an Angel's breath. Whilst Jacquie knows the book will never be read by the women who went before her, she hopes that her daughter and grand-daughters will enjoy this collection of tales in years to come.

It may be a hand-me-down but they could read it in their search for their own   four   leaf   clover!

Jacquie and The Irene's